I0585463

VOSS

The Price of Innocence

VOSS *The Price of Innocence*

Copyright 2018 ©Terry L Probert

First published in Australia in 2018 by Probert Consulting

All rights reserved. No part of this publication may be reproduced, stored in a retrieval system, or transmitted in any form or by any means, electronic, mechanical, photocopying, recording or otherwise, without the prior written permission of the publisher. Nor may it be published, or otherwise circulated, in any form of binding or cover other than that in which it has been published.

All characters in this publication are fictitious and any resemblance to any person living or dead is purely coincidental.

Cataloguing in Publication Data is available from the Australian National Library.

ISBN: (trade paperback) 978-0-9874074-4-3

ISBN: (E-publishing version) 978-0-9874974-5-0

Website: www.wurugi.blogspot.com.au
Trade enquiries: probertconsulting@bigpond.com

Cover design: End 2 End Books
http://www.end2endbooks.co/

Editing: Merlene Fawdry mfawdry@bigpond.net.au

Printing: IngramSpark

One can absorb much from theory, however it's the repetition of doing, that creates skill.

For my family

VOSS

The Price of Innocence

Terry L Probert

CHAPTER ONE

The woman was on her knees, her wrists bound with cable-ties and hogtied to those around her ankles. Her face gone, just a bit of skin and bone held in place by the gag. One shot, probably a dum-dum to the back of the head, had exploded and spread her brain, the very thing that made her Estelle, across the white tiles and onto the designer couch. I knew it was her, our names joined by a heart still tattooed on her shoulder. I smiled to myself, it must have pissed him off that she'd never removed it.

I hadn't seen her since our divorce sixteen years before, not in the flesh anyway. I'd see her face sometimes as I flipped past the social pages to get to the sports section. Estelle had always wanted more than I could give her but, even after an ugly divorce and wallowing in my darkest mood, I couldn't see how she deserved this.

Luke Peter's death had been slower. The positioning of their bodies showing she'd been forced to watch the slow torture of her husband. The passive prick had probably been too soft to put up a fight. Gabby Stringer, the Medical Examiner, found no defensive wounds. It was as if he'd just let whoever had done this tie him to the chair and begin the carving.

'Died a death of a thousand cuts,' Gabby said. She looked drawn and way too old for her thirty two years. 'Each cut no deeper than four millimetres, except for the last one,' she pointed, 'and that's the one that killed him.' A gash had opened along the side of his neck and followed the carotid artery. 'It's not deep and the bruising shows that they used a different blade. This was torture.' She stood, put her hands in the middle of her back and stretched. Gabby took time to look around the room. 'Nice place to die.'

'No one needs to die like this,' I said.

'Sorry Voss, did you know them?'

'A long time ago, Gabby.' I suppressed a sigh, 'it was a lifetime ago.'

Forensic officers were picking their way through every room, the continual flash from their cameras adding to my headache. Apart from the murder room, the whole place had been trashed. Original art works had been ripped from the walls and scattered like discarded chip wrappers, broken frames rendered to kindling. In the bedroom, an antique dresser stood stripped of its drawers, contents strewn across the room. I picked up a woman's pullover and put it to my nose. It smelled of her perfume and I could feel Estelle in everything. I put it back. The corners of the carpets had been ripped back. These weren't just any intruders, whoever had done this was looking for something, but I guessed Peters and Estelle were well dead by then.

I moved to the bedside table, picked up the phone and checked the last call to the house. I knew the number. Estelle's mother had often called me when she couldn't reach her only child. Telling Donna, a woman who had been more of a mother to me than anyone I'd ever known, was going to be difficult. It was something I needed to do alone.

Closing my eyes, I tried to imagine the house before tonight. I went to the kitchen, dirty dishes in the washer showed they had dined on lasagne, followed by tiramisu. Estelle loved cooking Italian. If I'd been a gambling man, I could have wagered a week's pay on that menu and won.

It was her Sunday specialty. An officer tapped me on the shoulder and I turned to see.

Sir.' He held up the cutlery draw so I could see it from underneath. A zip-lock bag was taped to the underside. Inside it, a leather key-fob holding a brass key.

'Better bag it.' I was abrupt, but I knew that key-fob. It had once swung from the key that fitted the front door of our first home. Not anymore though, I'd sold the place and moved into a rented duplex closer to work until I found a passion for cars, ex-police cars, and moved to a place with enough space to accommodate them.

I opened the fridge door, looking for answers that I knew were not in this house. I slammed it shut, said goodbye to Gabby and headed for Luke Peters' office.

After I'd received Donna's call, I sent a patrol out to check the Peters' place. It hadn't been necessary. An hour before their security service had called to report a break in, however they had no CCTV vision. The outside security cameras had been smashed, possibly shot out, spray cans had been used to blank out those inside the home. The killer or killers had either disabled the alarms or got one of the victims to do it. They were dead by the time the scheduled patrol arrived.

Until now, Luke Peters QC had worked from his chambers in the court district. He also kept an office close to the restaurant area in Canberra Central, as a place to meet the more common crim. He was not seen as exclusive and took work where he could. I'd often heard him brag that mob bosses had to come from somewhere, so if you got them young you could keep them for life. Only this time, that life had been his. Why he died and who had done it, was now my problem.

I called my superintendent while I drove over there. I assured her that although I knew the victims, I'd had no contact for years. She wanted me to pass the case over to another team, but I insisted on following it. After her usual warnings and my assurances, I kept the case. I could not have cared less about who killed Peters, the list of mob bosses and small time crims who might have a grudge was a long one. Estelle's murder was different, but no more than any other wife forced to witness her partner's murder.

Forensics had secured his office and were busy boxing files when I arrived. I spent twenty minutes with his secretary, Tamsyn, but she knew, or was saying little about possible enemies. There had been an altercation with a cyclist who keyed his car last year, but that had been resolved. After hearing the story, I sympathised with the bloke on the bike, but took his contact details anyway.

Tamsyn said she scanned everything that came through the post or fax and downloaded it onto their database. The computers backed up at eight o'clock every night. If we compared the files with the database, we'd soon know if anything had been taken. She thought it would be easy.

'Anyone else use this office?' I asked.

Tamsyn wriggled in her chair and went all dumb blonde on me. 'No, it's only me and Mr Peters. Most of the time though, it's only me.'

'Does the practice have a Facebook page?' I looked around. The place was elegant and I could see Estelle's style in the furniture and fittings. 'Or other social media, you know, web page, etcetera?'

Tamsyn squirmed again. 'We have a website, but it's pretty basic.' She passed me a card with her photo and the company details on it. I flipped it over, a line of alternate contact numbers in raised black font against a white background directed you to the right person if the matter was urgent, 'I wouldn't think Luke would do Twitter or Facebook.'

'Do you do Twitter or Facebook?' I pushed my pad across the desk without waiting for an answer. 'Make a list. Better include any websites or blogs too?

'Some are,' her face flushed, 'well, they're a bit racy. You know the type. The ones I wouldn't like Mum or my boyfriend to know about.'

'Better write every one of those down too, the people you work for and how I can get hold of them.'

From a knock-off designer bag, or maybe it was real, she produced an old fashioned address book. It took time, but I had a list.

'This is just between us, yeah?'

'Look Tamsyn, right now you're a witness in a murder enquiry, your boss and his wife are dead. I'll try to keep your secrets, but no promises, okay?'

'I can't believe they're dead?' She flopped onto her arms and sobbed. I thought it contrived but asked a female officer to comfort her and take down anything she had to say, while I drove out to speak with Estelle's mother.

The meeting with Donna was difficult and added nothing to my view of what was happening in the Peters' lives. I offered what comfort I could and left feeling inadequate against the first rush of her grief. It was just on dark when I arrived home. Eddie, the homeless guy who'd taken to living in my yard, was scrunched between the hedge that bordered the grass, and my row of Mr Lincoln roses. I didn't disturb him, just hit the garage door remote and drove inside. I was home in an empty house, longing for an empty mind.

CHAPTER TWO

I set the oven, pulled a frozen pizza from its packet and left it on the sink. While the oven came up to temp I spread a tray with oven fry chips and waited. I knew I should be eating healthier but after today, this was all I could manage. I thought about Eddie and grabbed an extra plate from the cupboard. He probably needed feeding more than me. My fridge, like many I'd seen when investigating a murder, suggested this place belonged to some sad individual who lived on his own, sustained by a diet of ready meals.

Two lonely tomatoes rolled in the bottom of the crisper. I grabbed them, a celery stalk and a carrot. I saved what I could from a browning lettuce, fashioned a salad of sorts and dumped a serve on each plate. I slid the pizza and chips into the oven, grabbed a couple of beers and went around to the side yard. After I nudged him with my left foot, Eddie crawled out of his cocoon.

His face was held together by greying skin that supported eyes hidden so deep in their sockets, it was hard to tell their colour. From our first acquaintance years before, I remembered he had one blue and one green eye so, even apart from his current habitat, he'd always had his differences. I passed him the bottle and he cupped it as one would a hot cup of soup on a cold day.

'Ta,' he said, 'you good?'

'Yep, you?'

'So, so.' His eyes scanned my face and I could see their colour now. 'Tough day at the office though, I can see that.'

'Yeah,' I said. A part of me wanted to share, but how do you trust someone whose own trust has been eroded, 'I knew her.'

'Want to talk?' He thrust his empty bottle at me.

'Nope.'

I took the bottle and left mine on the step. It would be empty by the time I returned. Eddie wasn't a drunk, I knew that much. He was more an opportunistic drinker. I provided and he drank. Inside the kitchen I opened the oven and turned everything. I grabbed two more bottles from the fridge and padded outside again. Eddie had shrugged off his bedding and was sitting on the step. I edged around him and sat down. He took the beer.

'You ever gunna do anything about all this?' I more waved than pointed to his sparse belongings.

'You want me gone?'

'I didn't say that.' I heard the defence in his tone and wanted to reassure him he could stay. He was the best security system I'd ever had. 'I've told you, if you clean up you can move inside. You know where the spare key is'

'Yeah, but I'm okay like this.'

He'd once been the bloke who'd had it all, an eighties electronics whizz kid who'd made it in property development. I'd enlisted his aid in solving a cyber-fraud case a couple of years later. Last I'd heard of him was that he'd rode the crash out in the nineties, but the GFC smashed him. I had hardly given him a thought until seven months ago when I came home to find him sitting in the front of the house. I didn't recognise him at first, but he looked like he needed a feed and some new clothes. After an enforced shower, a meal, and one of my tracksuits, I'd dropped him off at the Salvos.

A week later he was back again. This time he'd pitched a tent, almost hidden between the bottlebrush hedge and the gate to the sideway. I could see he'd taken a severe beating and I wanted to take him to hospital, but he said he'd cope. I hadn't recognised him at first and thought he looked like a derelict who had gotten into a fight over booze or something. I wanted to ask, why he'd chosen my place to settle, but let it go. This bloke had fallen so far and I wasn't about to rub it in with questions he may not want to answer. I thought he'd hang around for a day or two while he licked his wounds and then he'd be gone. I'd been wrong.

Once when I asked why he didn't go home, he said he'd just dropped out. Whenever I pushed, he put up barriers and after a while I backed off.

I'd offered to help him find a place several times, but he'd waved the suggestion away and I let it rest. He could stay in the tent out of sight of the street. It had suited me to have someone to watch over my shed full of cars at the back of the house, until today. Now it was payback time as I needed his expertise for this case.

'Don't you ever want your old life back?'

Whatever Eddie was hiding from could wait until he was ready to share. 'What for? You work your arse off and all you do is make money for someone else.' His eyes had moved to the front of their sockets and I wondered what memories lit their fire. 'If I did it over, I'd leverage better. Spend more time with my family. If I'd done it properly back then, I might know where they are now. Hell, they might even care where I am now,' he looked across the roofs and out to the mountains, 'they might've even looked for me.' He slapped the step. 'Fuck 'em though, it's all wasted now anyway.' I noticed even the language of the streets couldn't mask the refinement in a voice that spoke of better times.

'What about I link you into some services?'

'Why?' he pushed both empty bottles at me.

'So you can come inside, get on with life.'

'I never liked being inside. That's what made me so good at what I did. Always on the edge, I never conformed, Sam, I never conformed.'

I stood up. 'Well I don't want to find you dead from exposure on my front porch when I come home one day, that's all.'

'Tell you what, mate, I'll move next door and die in old misery gut's garden if I feel it coming on. That'd suit you yeah?' He half stood to move position, tracksuit pants hanging lower than they should and between his shirt and the loose elastic of the waistband, I saw his skin sag. It reminded me of a mechanic's rag.

'C'mon Eddie, dinner's nearly ready. What do you want to drink?'

'Let's give that beer another try, eh? I'm beginning to get a taste for it.'

I balanced our meals on one arm and carried the beer in my right hand. Eddie had no use for cutlery, so it was fingers tonight.

My phone vibrated in my pocket and I stood and went inside as I answered. Teasing the venetian blind apart I looked out at Eddie. He had both plates on his knees. My dinner was done.

By eight o'clock I was inside an inner city apartment. I recognised the clothes and hair. One glance was all I needed to know it was Tamsyn. Someone had worked on her hard, tried to beat something out of her was my guess. Her young face now no more than pulp. Gabby from the coroner's office had arrived and the forensic team were already processing the scene.

'Computer hard drive and her phone are missing,' an officer said, pointing to chargers cables left behind, and I nodded to let him know I'd heard him.

Gabby looked up at me. 'Got any ideas on the Peters yet?'

'Nope, but I'm thinking I'd like a decent meal without it being interrupted.'

'You asking me out, Voss?'

God, where did that come from, 'Sorry no, I was just thinking about my half-eaten pizza being devoured by the vagrant who lives in my front yard.'

'So, you wouldn't ask me out then?'

'Sorry, yeah I'd love to have a meal with you sometime, it's just...'

She held her hand up. 'It's okay, I was only teasing.'

I understood. With her job you needed to inject a bit of humour sometimes.

She began half humming, half singing, *Not Pretty Enough*, by Kasey Chambers. If the case wasn't enough to drive me crazy, Gabby's singing was and we looked at each other and smiled, there'd be no other humour in this place.

The unit had been trashed. I took my time to take it all in as I walked through. The intruders had left the scene in the same manner as that of the Peters' place. Nothing left in a drawer, box or bag, contents littering the rooms. Whatever they wanted, they either found last, or Tamsyn hadn't known about it.

Her music collection had been dumped on the floor. I pulled my gloves on and turned over a compact disc that stood out from the rest. It was either a demo, or one downloaded from the internet. Someone had scrawled, *Tamsyn's Beat Mix, May 2016* with a black marker, so I assumed it was party songs. I bagged it as evidence, I thought I'd have it copied and listen to in the car later. It might help me get an insight into who Tamsyn really was.

A knock on the doorjamb caught my attention and I looked up to see Lucy Nguyen, my newly promoted Detective Sergeant, letting me know she had arrived.

'Penny for them, sir?'

She came further into the room and flicked through the scatter of discs with her pen.

'There are a lot that don't match their covers, but only this one is a generic disc and I can't find its cover.' I held up the bag, asking myself as much as her, 'Why?'

'Because it's a DVD.' She looked around the room, 'the television has a player; do you want me to try it?' She held out her hand and I passed it over.

She turned on the modest flat-screen and waited for it to start. Another disc was in the slot. Taking it out, she examined it and said. 'That's weird, the television should be able to read it.'

Before I dropped it into another evidence bag, I turned it over and held it to the light. The burn had only taken about a third of the area. 'I reckon it's meant to look like something it's not. Take them both back to work and have them checked on the computer. See what you can come up with, or get the techies to look at it.'

'Sure, what am I looking for?'

'You'll know when you find it.'

'Voss.' Gabby called me into the kitchen, where she dangled another evidence bag in front of me. 'Look familiar?' She jiggled it again. 'Care to guess where it's from?'

'Nope.'

Looking at it and then back to me, she gave me that know it all smirk she often used. 'I reckon it fits the same lock as the one we found taped under the drawer at the Peters' place, but this time we have an address.'

I took the bag and looked at the key tag showing it belonged to an industrial estate to the east of Canberra.

'Lucy,' I called back to the other room, 'you're with me.'

'What about the DVD?'

'Later. Pull some beak away from their dinner. Ask them for a warrant and have it emailed to your phone?'

Half an hour later, we drove down a side street and into an industrial site in Fyshwick. The place was grey, unimposing from the street, and the blank hoarding on the front kept its identity a secret. A security logo offered an emergency number. Lucy called it and after a few minutes the gate glided open. She couldn't glean the security code from them but, before we'd parked, one of their patrol units pulled in behind us.

'Brad.' His mouth was full of something as he pointed to the name on his jacket. He puffed his way to the door and we followed.

'I'll get the alarm,' he said and worked his key in the lock. He stepped in and punched a code into the panel. 'One, two, three and four.'

The alarm disabled, he flicked a switch to bring the foyer lights on.

Lucy smiled at me and said, 'You'd reckon they could do better than that.'

Brad just shrugged. 'Lucky you caught me grabbing a bite.' He shook his head and used his palm to rub crumbs from his shirt, 'I was just around the corner.'

'What happens here?' I asked as Lucy tried the evidence key in the lock. It turned.

'Dunno,' he said. 'I just get to check the joint from the outside. Most of the time I just reset the alarm when it goes off.'

'When it goes off? You don't come in and take a look around? Just reset the alarm?' I was annoyed and my tone was sharper than I'd intended. 'Sorry, it's been a long day.'

He finished chewing and swallowed. 'Not exactly. I check the outside and I wait in the foyer here until the bloke in a silver Mercedes arrives. He usually has a heavy with him. They go inside and I get back to my rounds. Security cameras capture everything that happens outside, the roof and perimeter, but we,' he pointed at the logo on his jacket, 'don't get to see inside.' He shrugged. 'It's not military, not government and not bikies, so your guess is as good as mine.' He went to a switch panel and flicked every light on. 'I'll leave you to it then?'

'This bloke in the Mercedes,' I said, 'do you know what he does?'

'Nope, but the heavy with him is real creepy. He's got sleeves on both arms and a bloody great cobra tattoo that winds its way around his neck. It goes all the way to the top of his head. He's so tall and ripped that I reckon he has to spend a heap of time in the Gym.'

'Thanks.'

Brad wriggled his way behind the steering wheel of a car at least two sizes too small and we watched him leave before going inside. I closed the door behind us as Lucy drew her weapon. I frowned and she re-holstered it.

'Bit jumpy?' I asked.

'Place gives me the creeps, Voss. Have you worked out what it is yet?'

'A set for stick movies?'

Pulling a pair of gloves on she said, 'I reckon you're right.'

I did the same. 'Get on to base and have them run a check on the address. Find out who owns the place. I don't see the Estelle I knew being mixed in something like this. I guess her husband had to put his money somewhere, but porn? I'm not so sure about that.'

'Might be why she left you Voss, wanted more and you weren't there.'

Today, more than ever the barb stung. She may have been right, but I was not about to admit it.

'Any news on that owner yet?' I snapped the question.

We spent another hour looking at the various pieces of equipment on the film sets. I'd seen my share of porn, but some of this stuff was more than kinky and just looking at it made me want to wash. Lucy must have picked up on my discomfort early and her comments only made it worse.

'You right to catch a lift back with someone from uniform?' I asked.

'Yeah, I want a better look around anyway.'

I just wanted to get out of there.

Arriving home, I found Eddie still in the garden. Our plates had been rinsed and left on the sink to drain. He'd locked the door and retired for the night. Everything was still and above the whisper of the city I could hear him. His snoring solicited an occasion growl from the neighbour's poodle but it seemed, as far as he was concerned anyway, all was right with the world. That was until I found his note stuck to the fridge, it reminded me to buy beer tomorrow.

CHAPTER THREE

Something about Estelle haunted me and I couldn't sleep. It wasn't the fact that she was dead, or remembering how she'd left me. This felt more sinister, more primal. I fell asleep, only to wake at four a.m. wide awake and needing to talk to someone. With only Eddie around, he would have to do. I went outside and used my foot to push at the crumple that wrapped him, nudging until he woke.

'Inside, now,' I ordered. 'I've put a towel, shampoo and a razor in the bathroom, clothes in the spare room. Not the latest, but they'll do.'

'Are you arresting me for eating your pizza?' He was still half asleep.

'No, I'm telling you that you're better than this, mate.' I waved my hand over his bedding, a combination of sleeping bag and blankets. He'd pulled the latter over his eyes, but I felt my gesture had been worth it. 'You need to shower and start working.'

A slit appeared where I imagined his eyes to be. 'What? Get back onto the great hamster wheel of progress and keep running till I'm all burnt out and as miserable as you. You know where you can stick that.' He pulled the opening closed.

'If I have to, then everyone else does too, and you're no exception.'

He opened his cocoon enough for me to see his face this time.

'It took me years to find out that this working lark is just bullshit. All created by politicians to keep the working man at heel.' Again he pulled the bedding over his head and turned away.

I tried again. 'Well I don't see why I have to bust a gut and you don't. Jeeze Eddie, I see your copies of *The Financial Review* in the recycling when I put the bin out. So don't expect me to believe you still don't long for the chase,' he stirred and I felt encouraged to go on. 'The thrill of closing that next big deal. C'mon, blokes like you live for making something out of nothing. And Eddie,' I rocked his shoulder with my foot again, 'I'll bet London to a brick you don't see yourself as being this homeless philosopher living on my goodwill forever, either. You know it's all bullshit, too.'

I squatted on my haunches and tugged at his blankets. He rolled away.

'Yeah, you might drink my beer,' I said, 'but there are never any extra bottles or evidence of drugs. If you were into that, you wouldn't be living in the side garden of a broken down, bitter and twisted cop like me.'

My blood was up and I wondered if I should stop and apologise. The thought passed. 'No mate,' I tried to open his blankets again, 'you might be down now, but I'll bet you're always planning your way out of this fucking hole.' I pushed him a little harder and he groaned. 'So, my little feral friend, from now on, if I have to go to work each day, so do you.'

'Piss off, Voss.' He opened a hole in his bedding and looked at the sky where the stars were still out. 'What time is it?'

'A bit after four thirty.'

'Piss off, I certainly don't need a lecture from you, or anyone else at this time of the day.' He retreated further into his bedding.

I crouched down and ripped the covers from his face. 'Think about it Eddie,' I had my hand inches from his face and rubbed my thumb and forefingers together, 'I'll advance you the cash, enough for you to get back in the business, but not until you've helped me crack this case.'

'Where, when, why?'

'Here, because that's where we are. When? Now, because it's what I do and why? Because she was someone I knew a very long time ago.'

'So it's personal. Who?'

'Yes it's personal, very personal.' Even though it was a lifetime ago, I could see Estelle's face reflected in every window and shiny surface again. 'My ex-wife.'

'You should have said.'

'Too hard.' I turned my back to him.

'What time is it again?'

'Time you were clean. Come on get yourself into that shower.' I saw him move, only to pull the cover back over his face again.

'Aw piss off, Voss. You know I can't do that shit anymore.'

'Look, Eddie, now I'm begging you, and you know I don't do that,' I felt an urge to let my anger rise, but tempered it. 'Listen, arsehole... I'm just not equipped with the right smarts for this one,' I felt my words drag. 'I need your brain. You understand numbers, you see trends and stuff, right?'

His face was out of the sleeping bag again. 'Yeah, I love a spread sheet, so what?'

I thought I saw his eyes twinkle, but the vacant stare was back before I could be sure.

'Come on Eddie, what do I have to do to get you to say yes?'

'Probably put a gun to my head?'

'Listen, I just need someone from outside the force to run an eye over Luke Peters' accounts and tell me in simple terms what's in there. You don't have to ask why, just do it, please.'

He wriggled part way out of his bedding. 'I get to stay in the house.'

'Only if you shower.'

'I have to shower?' He made it sound as if I was infecting him with the black plague, but I sensed a joke in there somewhere. He stood up and pulled the sleeping bag around him.

'Every day and you have to keep the place tidy.'

'But I get to live inside?'

'We share the house.' I pointed at the front door. 'You sleep in the spare room. On the left at the back, French doors open onto the garden.'

I thought I had him until he said, 'Sorry Sam, not in a hundred years.' The Sam was a giveaway. He usually only used it when he wanted to get up my nose. I watched him squat down and wriggle into the depression he'd made in his bedroll. I tried again, but our conversation had ended. I went inside, picked up my gear and went to the car, Eddie may not need breakfast, but I did. Somewhere in this town, a fast food restaurant would be serving plastic breakfasts to poor sods like me.

When I arrived at work just after seven, the Superintendent's car was in the parking lot. It made me uneasy as most days she didn't get in until around eight. I looked around the parked cars, the rest of my crew weren't in yet. Not that they were late, but they weren't early either. I felt pleased as it would give me a chance to catch up on their reports before the hustle of the day began.

I walked straight to my office, closed the door, hung up my jacket, threw my keys onto the desk and leaned my backside against it. Through the dividing windows I stared at the photos on the incident board in the outer office. Little wonder no-one was in, they'd worked until midnight by the look of it. I turned back to the notes on my desk, picked up a report from Lucy and started skimming it when the door opened. The boss walked in.

'Looks like hell broke loose yesterday,' she said. 'You okay, Voss?

'Sure,' I thought she was about to admonish me but changed her mind. 'She was a world ago.'

'Yes, but?'

I interrupted her. 'Ma'am, I have no issues other than wanting to solve the murder of Estelle... and Slippery. 'It's what I do.'

'Hang on, Voss. All I'm saying is that I can put another officer on the case and you take some leave, just until this is over.' She put her hands back and slid up onto my desk. I moved away. 'Slippery eh, never heard him called that.'

'Sorry, an old habit. I never got over the prick backdooring me.'

'And you never strayed? Why Voss, I'm surprised?'

Una knew me as well as anyone, so I didn't rise to her tease. 'I took my marriage seriously, more seriously than Estelle, but she didn't need to die like that.' I handed her a wad of photos from the crime scene.

She started flicking through them. 'Okay, but if things get rough and you need some time...'

'I understand, Ma'am.'

'For Christ's sake, Voss. I must have told you to call me Una a hundred times.'

'But these days, you're my superior Ma'am and I know my place.' I couldn't tell her I didn't like the name. It always brought a vision of some fusty great aunt and this Una was anything but that. I remembered her telling me that her parents had chosen the name for its Gaelic meaning, "she knows", and me laughing, knowing that they'd got it right.

The team were filing into the outer office now and she took this as her cue to leave. She nodded greetings as she passed and more than one pair of eyes watched expensive stockings in expensive shoes carry this high maintenance woman to her office. Una Knight may be a superintendent of police, but she still knew how to draw attention her way.

I walked out to Lucy and handed her the file.

'Trouble sir?'

'Not for me.' I said.

'But for someone?'

I let her comment go and walked to the incident board. 'Right, what have we got?'

Over the next hour we thrashed out which leads to prioritise. I set and delegated tasks and later, back in my office, I took the copies of the two discs from Tamsyn's unit, saved them to a flash drive and slipped it into my pocket. I was still going over the forensic reports when Lucy Nguyen tapped on my open door.

'Sir, we've got another one.'

I grabbed my phone and tossed her my keys. 'C'mon, you can drive.'

CHAPTER FOUR

When we arrived at the scene, emergency services were in full swing and the clean-up crew were diverting traffic. A Black BMW M6 coupe had cut a swathe across the verge and wrapped itself around a tree. Gabby was already packing her kit.

I pulled my gloves on, 'What have we got?'

She passed me the victim's wallet, 'Rory Adderton, thirty-three years old. A bullet to the head made sure he'd died long before the car crashed. Cruise control was set.' She held up an insurance company data logger and wiggled it. I figured it was an attempt to make sure I saw it. 'We'll download the car's data, but my guess is he died about five hundred metres back.'

'Bullet entered where?'

She pointed to the front of the vehicle. 'Through the windscreen, got him about a centimetre above the eyes. I doubt if he even saw the screen craze.'

I passed the wallet to Lucy and she grabbed her phone as she walked away. I knew she'd already started digging into the victim's life. I walked back along the freeway to where Gabby had thought the bullet hit him, squatting to assume the driver's seated position. I scoured the horizon and looked for landmarks to reference my position. I walked back toward the crash scene, about six hundred metres before it I stopped. The road rose and eased to the left, a few native shrubs clumped on the inner edge of the corner. I phoned Lucy and asked her to meet me. The verge had been mowed a few weeks before and I figured it must have rained since, as new grass was now about seventy millimetres above the stubble. Between the bushes we found a spot where something had flattened the unmown grass. I dropped down onto my belly, shuffled around until I found holes in the dirt the sniper had used to set his elbows and mimed holding a rifle. 'The shot came from here.' I stood up and brushed myself down. 'They're right handed.'

'Like you,' Lucy said, dragging out her phone and calling forensics to instruct them to widen their search. When she finished the call, the phone went back into her pocket. 'You're sure the shooter propped here?' She pretended to sight a rifle and pull the trigger. 'It would be a great shot.'

'Unless you're the driver.'

'Well, there is that.'

I'd seen enough. It was time to find if there was a link to the Peter's case. 'Let's go back and start rattling some chains.'

For the next three hours we drilled deep into Adderton's history, but didn't find any links to Estelle or Luke Peters. My instincts told me there was a connection and my frustration built. Desperate for some space to think, I headed upstairs to tell the boss we had two separate cases, my last chore before I went home. Una again offered to replace me and again I refused.

I left the office without saying goodbye, not something I usually did, but today, part of my mind was on Eddie too. Apart from on the spot home security, I'd never thought about why I'd allowed him to hang around for so long. Perhaps my subconscious knew I'd need him for a case such as this. Whatever the reason, I decided it was time for him to either help or ship out. While I drove, my mind switched back to the shooting on the highway. How could the assailant be sure they would make the shot and if they did, how would they know their victim was dead. I started to wonder if anyone in the morning's traffic had noticed anything. I was driving on instinct, not really seeing much other than the cars around me. Without thinking, I swung into my drive and grabbed the remote to raise the garage door before I snapped out of my daze. Eddie had gone. I stopped the car, got out and went to the spot in behind the roses where he spent much of his time. The mulch had been dragged smooth. My garden was back to how it had been before he arrived. I looked around, scanning the neighbours' yards, thinking he may have moved on, but he wasn't there.

Stuff him and all of his crap. In a couple of days, I'd forget he'd ever been here. I kicked at the mulch and walked over to check the letter box. It was empty. I went back to the car, opened the garage door and drove in. A dirty Buzz Lightyear backpack and Eddie's swag and the paraphernalia of his homeless state were by the rear roller door. I thought it strange, but figured he'd just stashed it here for a while.

I locked the car and walked to the door leading to the living room. Something seemed different and I didn't get my head around it at first. The radio was playing and cooking smells wafted from the kitchen.

'You're late.' It was Eddie's voice, but my mind wasn't moving as fast as the sensory information it was taking in.

I shook my head, took stock of what was happening and as if expected, asked, 'What's for dinner?'

'That's bloody lovely, here I am stuck at home keeping house, while you're out saving the world,' his pout reminded me of Puss in the second Shrek movie, 'and all you want to know, is what's for dinner?' He turned his cheek out. 'Not even a kiss, or hello darling, I'm home.'

He slapped a tea towel over one shoulder and glared at me. 'Nothing. Sam, it's just not good enough.'

Not many people called me by my first name and it sounded weird coming from him. For a second or two I didn't know what to think, but soon reckoned two could play his game. 'Well, what is it?' I said and leant in, pretending to kiss him.

'Rack off.' He ducked away, laughing. 'I was just kidding. Try to kiss me again and I'll break your nose.'

'Call me Sam again and I'll break more than your nose, so tell me, what we've got?' The smell was making my mouth water.

'You like Italian?' His grin flashed and was gone.

My mind jumped to Estelle and hoped he hadn't made lasagne.

'Love it.'

'Well you're out of luck. I found enough stuff to cobble a poor man's pasta together. It'll be food, but not as you know it.' His face and hands were clean, but he still stood in rags, and he stank. 'After dinner we negotiate.' he said.

'Before dinner, you shower. Then we eat, and then we negotiate.'

He turned back to stir his sauce, as if giving my ultimatum consideration, before turning back to me, spitting in his palm and shaking hands on the deal. I walked to the kitchen tap and washed my hands before setting the table.

I'd just lifted the lid to check the sauce, deciding it looked as good as it smelled when he re-entered the room minus the seven years of grime and rough living that was now running down my drain, although the facial hair was still intact.

As if reading my thoughts, he reacted defensively, 'Don't blame me, I never use another man's razor.'

He fiddled with a pot of boiling water. 'The gnocchi's a bit rough. I made it from scraps and whatever else I could salvage.' He opened and closed the fridge door and let out the sort of sigh you hear when a parent is frustrated with a child. 'No parmesan, Voss, you're a bloody embarrassment.'

After dinner, I hunted down a disposable razor while Eddie cleaned the kitchen then, when he went off to the bathroom to shave, I excused myself on the pretext of making a call. I went into the garage, dragged his bedding into the back yard and loaded most of it into the fire pit. His Buzz Lightyear backpack I saved and placed by the French doors. A slosh of lawnmower fuel soaked the mess that had been his home since he'd dropped out. I went to toss a match at it and a thought knocked on the door of my conscience. Should I ask him if he wanted to make something of a ceremony out of it? I reconsidered and the match did its work. Eddie, the derelict, was no more.

When I went back inside, he was clean shaven and in place of a hedge of unruly hair, he had combed it back and fashioned it into a plait. My planned image of a new Eddie hadn't been the one standing in front of me.

'You scrub up okay.' My clothes just hung from him like those on an under stuffed scarecrow and I tried to stifle my laugh. 'They just need taking in a bit.'

'Gunna be bloody hard to put weight on living here though, eh?' He held the fridge door open and stared into it like a dog gawping at an empty bowl. 'Not much of a one for cooking, are you?'

'Nope.'

'You did say board and lodgings?'

'McDonalds might have to do?'

'Rack off Voss, I might as well be back on the street.'

'Or go hungry, your choice.'

'We'd better go to the supermarket then?'

'When?'

'Now.'

'Fine.' I was beginning to regret my offer.

Eddie opened the pantry and checked the freezer. He slid open the drawer under the stove and checked my utensil rack. 'We've got a bit to buy, Sam. When do you get paid?'

'End of the month, why?'

'There's no damn food here and nothing to cook with anyway, that's why.' He looked around the kitchen a bit more. 'Okay I'm right now, let's go shopping but we may have to use your credit card.'

Next morning, I could hear Eddie snoring in the back room while I made my breakfast. I was tempted to call him, but reckoned as this was the first night for a long while since he'd slept in a decent bed, he could stay there. Having a stocked pantry had its benefits and I stood there holding the door open, spoilt for choice, I didn't know which spread to choose to put on my toast.

Breakfast finished, I put my plate into the dish washer and stashed the toaster away. I put three fifties and a note that said housekeeping under a magnet on the fridge and left.

A notice from forensics told me they'd found another key in the BMW. It too, fitted the warehouse. The cases were linked. It didn't matter if I felt like a fool for doubting my instincts, I needed to let Una know. She repeated her usual warnings about care and responsibility. I left before she finished.

The team still hadn't found the guys in the silver Mercedes who Brad had spoken about, so it was time to look for another connection to Rory. While Lucy drove out to his home address, I reread the report. Everything forensics had found suggested he lived on his own, but this place was devoid of anything homely. My guess was he used it as somewhere to send his mail. I instructed uniform to do another door knock of the neighbours. Forensics had the mail from yesterday, but I'd noticed a postman in the street when we drove up and decided to check the letterbox.

It held the usual contents. I put the junk mail back and held on to the bills. One caught my eye. It was from the same firm that patrolled the Peters' warehouse. Now we had something to follow.

West of the city, a sweaty man in his early sixties ushered us into a grubby office cramped into the corner of a concrete grey factory. Patrol vehicles were packed into every spare inch of the place. I guessed they only patrolled at night. He dried his hands on a towel that should have been laundered weeks ago and waved for us to sit down.

'Gotta keep 'em clean.' He pointed to the cars in the factory and threw the towel into the corner. 'Now, how can I help?'

I told him we had four murders and each one could be traced to the Peters' warehouse. Lucy gave him addresses we were interested in and he sorted through the data base on a desktop until he found Rory Adderton's details, which he printed off and handed to me. I put it on the desk and Lucy took a photo of both sides with her phone. He pulled Luke Peters' file too, and Lucy took it and followed the same procedure. I asked him to check the address for their house. He had nothing on that.

'We have another entry under the name of Peters,' he said, 'E Peters. I think it's a unit.'

Lucy took the printout and did the same as she had with the others.

'Can I have a quick look at your files?' I said.

'Yeah, no skin off my nose.'

'Thanks.' I said, as he turned the computer toward me. I flicked through from A to Z. Nothing of interest stood out.

We drove back to work with out talking, I guessed she was churning everything through her mind too. Mine was in overdrive making and remaking lists. At her station, Lucy started building her own database. I attended to everything in my in-tray and stopping at her desk, told her I had a few things to check. I would be back later.

It was time to put Eddie to work. I stopped off at Officeworks, bought a laptop, printer and an assortment of stationary supplies. When I arrived home the garage door was open and Eddie was giving the floor a sweep, moving the broom respectfully around my treasured Mini Cooper S. I walked toward him and again I noticed smells coming from the kitchen. This was becoming a habit I could get used to. He looked different too, his plait was gone and it looked as if held been dressed by Saint Laurent.

'I used a bit of the cash you left to clean up a bit,' he said, 'so, as a peace offering, I thought I'd better make biscuits.'

'And this?' I looked him up and down. A knitted fine wool grey sweater, covered a pink business shirt, designer faded blue jeans fitted as if they'd been tailored for him. He looked down and I noticed the shoes, soft Italian leather was my guess and he should have been able to see my smile in them.

'Vinnies and the Salvos. Gave it all a press, and here you have me, good as new.' He held his hands out and gave a twirl. 'What do you reckon, metrosexual or what?'

'You're full of surprises mate, but why the haircut?'

'You like?'

I neither liked nor disliked it, nor cared how much it cost him. He could have had a manicure too, for all I cared. None of it mattered at the moment, but I went along with his enthusiasm because I needed him on side. 'Here, I'll take a photo. Stand against the Mini.' I sorted through my phone to find the camera function.

'Why the photo?'

'Just in case you decide to slip back into dero mode. I'll have a reminder to drag you back with.'

'Won't happen.' He walked to the family room door and opened it, 'you don't know how long it's been since I had a place where I could cook. I hadn't realised just how much I've missed this.'

'So what's in the oven?'

'Beer-cake and chocolate chip cookies. Hope you've got a sweet tooth?' He held his grin and for the first time I had a good look at his teeth.

'You should do that more often.'

'Cook?'

'Nah, grin. Almost makes you human.'

'Piss off. Anyway, what are you doing home?'

'To put you to work. We found a couple of discs at a crime scene. I'm guessing photos and or data, but I want to know what's on them. I want you to tell me what it is, what it's about and where the data came from.' I loaded him up with the office equipment.

'Be okay to set up in here?' Eddie waved his arm at the empty car space.

'Why the garage? You don't want to use the study?'

'Why? There's more room, plus I can see out from here. I like to see who's around me before they see me. Gives me the advantage, you know? I'll drag in the outdoor table and use that.'

'If you're sure?' I slapped him on the back. 'Report on my desk tonight?'

'You don't have a desk, dickhead. I burnt it, along with all my stuff you left smouldering in the fire pit.'

'I wanted to tell you, but...'

'Bullshit, Voss. Like most cops, you're just trying to control me, that's all.' His teeth flashed again. 'I'm joking about the desk, but you should've asked.'

He was right, but I had work to do. 'There's a cordless phone in my bedroom, use that if you need to.'

I passed him my card, which he flipped over a couple of times. I pointed to the numbers. 'You can get me on either of these, okay?'

He shrugged and I turned to go back to the car.

'Better pick me up a mobile too,' he yelled at my back.

CHAPTER FIVE

Rory Adderton's file turned up a few minor convictions from his youth, but over the last fifteen years his record was clean. There were rumours around him and his business interests. We knew how people like him and his associates slipped through the system, but there was nothing worth chasing. He had surrounded himself with all the usual suspects, vice, drugs, money laundering, extortion, but we'd never found enough to charge him with.

Instinct told me he was connected to Luke Peters and I was that desperate for a connection, I could taste it. I wondered if Peters might have been on the take, but why had his torture been necessary? And if Estelle had known anything, she'd have said long before they killed her.

What had Peters been holding back or had he even known what they wanted?

I wondered about a secret so precious they were prepared to suffer and die for it. And at some point they must have known they were going to be murdered anyway.

Who were they protecting and why?

The questions kept going around in my mind. What was it that needed protecting?

My head pounded with a revolving door of questions.

In times of doubt I go to my training and set the team to follow the money. Tamsyn's bank account showed her salary from Peters' practice was transferred monthly. It wasn't a large wage, but a check of the award showed it was fair. Monthly transactions for rent were electronically transferred, as were her phone and university debt. There was nothing in this account to show why anyone would want her dead.

'Boss,' 'Lucy was leaning over a junior constable's desk pointing to the computer, 'check this out.'

Tamsyn's Facebook page was the usual claptrap of selfies and cat people, but one of her links took the viewer to a local travel writing blog. The constable had followed links to other sites and one website stood out. *Erotic Canberra.* A place where writers shared erotic stories She also traced her connections to several soft porn sites that advertised a raft of hard core connections. A video of a young woman popped up. She was doing a lot more than just entertaining two men.

'That's her? No wonder she was concerned about her mother finding out.' A crowd was gathering at the junior constable's desk, their sniggering understandable yet offensive.

'Constable, follow up on the boyfriend.'

'In Newman, Western Australia,' she said, 'fly in fly out worker, still got a week to go.'

'Okay the lot of you, back to work and... good work constable.' I said this loud enough for those around her to hear. It was only three little words, but I'd learned long ago that praise and encouragement reap bigger rewards than cracking the whip over your people.

'Sir,' Lucy was trying to get my attention, 'those names we took from her address book. I've cross referenced them with the database from the computers at movie-set, no matches.'

'Shit, shit, shit,' I said, it felt like every door we opened had a brick wall behind it. I took a moment to think and paced the room.

'Voss?' Her voice had an edge to it. 'Earth to Voss?'

I didn't let her break my concentration and I tapped the computer screen. 'Get someone checking those actor names against those on Tamsyn's Facebook page and any other website she visits or posts on. Check and cross reference everything. See if Rory Adderton comes up anywhere. He's the key to this, I can feel it.'

I stood in front of the incident board and pondered. After about ten minutes I went back to Lucy, who was now on the phone and waited for her to hang up.

'You wanted me?' I asked.

'Yes Sir,' she said, 'but it's okay, I just wanted your direction because I didn't want to double up, but I've gone ahead anyway. I've got someone checking who owns those IP addresses to find out how much of the stuff is bogus and how much of it's real.'

'Right,' I shook my head, trying to catch up with the pace of everything, 'good work.'

She picked up two stacks of paper and called a couple of junior officers together. I went back to the incident board and stood looking at nothing and everything, willing it to give up its secrets.

'Sir?' Lucy was alongside me, but I was deep in thought and barely heard her. I tried to fight my distraction and answer, but weakened to it again. She tried once more, 'Voss.' I knew she was there and waved at her to stop talking for a moment.

'The address book, was it in her apartment?'

'Sir?'

'Tamsyn's address book, did we find it?'

'I'll check.' Lucy said, picked up her phone and called forensics. She put her hand over the phone, 'they didn't find it.'

I was still thinking.

'Voss?' She was becoming impatient.

'Tell them to look again, turn her place and the office upside down if they have too.' My mind raced. 'That list she gave us, was Adderton's name on it?'

She let out a sigh, sifted through the stuff on her desk and ran a finger down the names. 'Not that I can see.'

'Find that address book and cross check his phone too. See if her number comes up,' I clapped my hands together to show the urgency required.

'Sorry,' she waved a hand as if trying clear her mind, 'I was just trying to get my head around it all.'

'Come on Lucy, that book might be the key to this. Get someone onto it now. When you find it, cross reference with his contacts.' Times like this, I felt as if I was trapped in quicksand with people around me doing nothing to get me out. I went to the front of the incident boards and raised my voice enough to address the room. 'Listen up, we all know most murders are solved in the first three days. Every hour after that makes the case more difficult. You all know what to do, so let's light a fire under it, eh?'

Something in Rory Adderton's background held the answer, I knew it. I went back to my office and sifted through a growing pile of papers waiting for my attention. I threw them back into the in-tray, administration could wait. I walked back to Lucy.

'Your car, five minutes.'

The carpark was deserted. I leant against the bonnet of Lucy's car and called Estelle's mother. She said Estelle and Luke's marriage had its share of ups and downs, but that had been seven years ago. Once they'd moved back to Canberra, Estelle and Luke had become the perfect couple. Estelle had a job with a fashion house, buying stock and running shows. She had an independent income and enjoyed the freedom it gave her.

Lucy jerked open the door of her car. 'Where to?'

'Lonsdale Street, Xirena Zelazny Designs.' I slid into the passenger seat and punched the address into the trip computer. A plastic voice could give Lucy her instructions. I used my phone to check their website, and then turned the screen for her to see.

'High end stuff,' Lucy said. 'No-one in my pay bracket could afford to shop there.'

'If there was one thing Estelle liked, it was high end.' My words came out louder than intended.

'Hard on the wallet was she, Sir?'

'Let's just concentrate on the job, shall we?' I probably owed Lucy more of an explanation, but not today.

I took out my smartphone to read though the list of Luke Peter's clients, memorised a few, and phoned the team to chase up their current contact details. By the time I'd finished, Lucy was parking the car in a no standing zone in front of Xirena Zelazny Designs. To me everything was over the top, but I'm not a woman.

'Close your mouth,' I said, 'we're here to work.'

Lucy walked to a mannequin and felt the fabric, looked at a label and turned it toward me.

'I do really love it darling,' she pouted. I cringed, but realised it was payback for my earlier attitude. 'You did say I could choose anything.'

If honey could talk, it would not have sounded any more cloying.

Within seconds, a woman in her early fifties was at my side. A gold badge on the lapel of her black jacket introduced her as Laurelle. Nothing like adding a fake French name to give the impression of class. If Estelle had had a hand in this, she hadn't given it a lot of thought.

'The tones would look wonderful on her, Sir. They really bring out the colour of her eyes.'

I showed my ID and introduced Lucy, Laurelle's enthusiasm waned.

Lucy explained the reason for our visit and I watched colour drain from the woman's face as Lucy rushed her to a chair. She knew little and after talking for half an hour, we'd learnt nothing new. She said Estelle breezed in and out on occasion, and I wondered if she lied when she told us she hadn't seen her for over six months. It wasn't hard for me to form an opinion of Laurelle as being little more than a shopgirl who ran the retail outlet, a shop girl with a secret. Maybe she fiddled the books. I didn't care. I knew we'd find out sooner or later.

I asked to look in the office and she waved me toward a door in what looked like a fashionable cupboard. I flicked through the incoming invoices and used my phone to photograph those of interest. I found the petty cash tin and opened it. The cash in the bottom was less than two hundred dollars. I studied the notebook the company used to balance the tin. Nothing unusual there, I closed it and put it back. When I tried to close the drawer, something jammed it. I shoved again and an envelope fell to the floor. Holding it under the desk lamp I could make out Adderton Insurance hand written on the front in a script similar to Estelle's. I tore open a corner and counted twenty, one hundred dollar notes,

I showed the envelope to Laurelle.

'How often does someone from Adderton Insurance call to collect?' I asked, passing the envelope to Lucy.

'Every two weeks.' She replied. 'I don't know the men. I just give it to them and hope they'll leave.'

'What do they look like?' Lucy had her pad out, pen poised.

'Big, scary.' She burst into tears. 'They're in and out. I just want them out of my shop as soon as possible.'

36

'Know anyone else they call on? Other retailers along this road?' Lucy said, she looked at me and smiled, I knew she'd glean whatever she could from Laurelle.

I went back into the office, made a few notes and then searched the store room. I found nothing out of the ordinary. I walked back to Laurelle and asked to check the till. She nodded. I opened it, checked the receipts tape and counted the cash. It matched. I lifted the plastic drawer liners and fanned through the warranty booklet and assorted pieces of paper. A scrap of paper with a Luke Peters header had hand written names and contact numbers for sales, accounts, warehouse and carriers. One lone number caught my attention. It didn't have a name, or a service attached to it. I waited for a break in Lucy's questioning to ask Laurelle who owned the number. She said it was for emergencies only and had never called it. Any trouble with customers or suppliers, she resolved herself. I took a photo and put it back. I slid the drawer out and set it on the counter. A purse sized address book was taped to the rear of the cavity. A quick look through and I recognised the names and private addresses of Canberra's good and the great. It was an old book, as the Assistant Commissioner's wife was listed under her maiden name. I asked Laurelle about the book, she claimed she'd never seen it. I took shots of each page and put it back.

When I looked up, Lucy and Laurelle were at the store's computer, the printer whirring. Lucy gave me a smile and winked. We had their client and suppliers list. I felt my phone vibrate and checked the screen. Una Knight. I ignored it.

Lucy's phone rang as we left the shop and I thanked the woman for her help, handing her my card before following Lucy to the car.

'That was the boss,' she said, 'it seems someone loved you after all.'

'What?'

'You told us to follow the money and now it's here to bite us,' she grinned at me, 'well you really.'

'What?' She wasn't making sense. I didn't do cryptic

'Sir, it appears that Estelle Peters made you a beneficiary to her estate.'

'What?' I rubbed a hand across my head and scrunched into the passenger seat, trying to absorb the information

Lucy pulled away as I tapped Adderton Insurance Services into Google. It was as I suspected, nothing came up.

'Go to the warehouse. We need to check something.'

'Sir, I'm to deliver you back to Superintendent Knight immediately.

'Drive to the warehouse.'

'Sir, I can't do that. She told me to arrest you if necessary, right now you're a suspect.'

CHAPTER SIX

I couldn't fathom why Estelle would make me a beneficiary of her estate. It didn't make sense. Her husband Luke, would have insisted she change her will once they were married. Lucy kept her eyes on the road and weaved through the afternoon traffic. I felt angry and wanted to lash out, but not at Lucy. She'd take the lead on the case now and I assumed her silence meant she was thinking about it.

'You ticked off?' I asked

'Not sure how to feel, how do I ask you...'

'Ask me what?'

'Well, I know you didn't kill her, or him, either. But I do want to know if you knew she'd named you in her will, and if so, did you try to hide it from us?'

'Lucy, I couldn't kill Estelle,' I felt an emotion rise, one I hadn't felt for years and I fought to keep it in check, 'I loved her...'

'And him?'

'I did my best to ignore the slippery bastard.'

'Not a fan then?'

'That doesn't make me his killer though.'

'What happens next?'

'Una Knight for me and a pile of problems for you. Maybe you could drop by the house every once in a while. You know, just to check that I'm not wallowing around in misery too much.'

'You know that can't happen. I can't tell you anything and whatever you do to tempt me won't get me to tell you anything, Voss.'

We drove the rest of the way in silence.

Lucy went to her desk. I went to my mine and called Superintendent Knight. She'd see me in my office the moment she was free. Her need to control worked to my advantage and I used the time to copy everything I could to a memory stick. I slid Adderton's file into the pile of papers in my in-tray and sat my briefcase on the return. I tidied the desk and walked to the incident room to check on the team's progress and absorb all I could before I was out of there.

I leant on Lucy's desk and studied the boards.

'Did they find the owners of the fashion house?' I could see one of the team had written the name up.

'Sir,' she slapped her pen down, 'you know I can't tell you anything, show you anything, or have you anywhere near this case. If you want to make yourself useful until the boss gets here, take these overtime sheets and sign them off.' She handed me a pile of paperwork and smiled. 'And while you're at it, sign these expense claims too.' The smile was beginning to look like a smirk.

I was miffed at being treated like a child, but pleased with Lucy's show of authority considering the sudden reversal of our roles. I wanted to drop my shoulders and sulk like a teenager, when something fell out of the file. The data logger from Adderton's car. I seized the chance to slip it into my pocket. 'Want me to drop in with these in the morning?' I waved the papers up and down, 'or do you want to pick them up on your way to work?'

'Come on Boss, you've got the time to do them now,' she pointed around the room with her pen, 'we all want to be paid this fortnight.' Her face had the appearance of stone and I wondered what was bothering her, but Una was bearing down like a ship headed for harbour.

'Voss, your office now.' Thinking her bellow was more bull than old cow, I smiled. It was a call I'd heard often, and as predictable as morning. I kept my face impassive, followed her in and closed the door behind us.

'Ma'am.' I held the visitor's chair out for her and sauntered to the other side of the desk to take mine. I was angry, but it was hard not to grin at her.

'Did you know about this?'

'Know about what exactly? I know you told Lucy to arrest me, but I'll be damned if I know why?'

'Cut the crap Voss. Did you know about Estelle's will?'

'I know about the wills Estelle and I had prepared when we were married, but I assumed that the moment she and Peters hooked up, they'd have written new ones.'

'This one is dated three months ago, Voss.' She crossed and re-crossed her legs, something she did when angry. 'You must have known?'

'No, Ma'am, it's news to me.' There was no point being mad, better to just get on with it. 'Your next question will be. Did I kill her? And you know I'm never going to answer that.'

'Listen, you may not have known about the will, but Luke Peter's brother has a fair bit of pull with the minister. He's demanding a quick resolution and reckons you're it.'

'They can whistle for all I care. Besides you've got nothing to hold me on,' people were watching us through the window from the outer office and I gave her a look to let her know we were under scrutiny, 'Ma'am'

She stood, lowered the venetians and snapped them shut.

'Jesus Voss, I know you didn't do it, you're not a killer,' she was agitated and I was heartened by this, 'but you and I both know that you can be the most exasperating man at times.'

I lifted an eyebrow and remembered the way she'd often dismissed opinions and suggestions of the three ex-husbands she'd kicked to the kerb, so stayed silent.

I was thinking about Peter Peters. The grasping little prick had a reputation for always being bailed out by his older brother and more than once he'd used his status to ingratiate himself with Canberra's upper crust. I didn't know what he did for a living, but his abilities couldn't match his life style. Una's mouth was still moving, but I wasn't listening.

She slapped the table. 'Are you even listening to me, Voss?'

'Sorry, I can't get over the fact that you're suspending me,' I grinned, 'it's a lot to take in.'

She leant across the desk and did something she hadn't done since our academy days, grabbing my face with both hands to make sure she had eye contact. 'Listen very carefully, for I will say this only once.' It wasn't the best parody of the woman of the resistance in Allo 'Allo, but it took me back.

She'd been the academy's golden girl and I'd been a klutz who hated paperwork. I don't know why she'd made it her personal mission to get me through, but she had and I was grateful for it.

She must have thought grabbing my face would emphasise the seriousness of the situation. Only this time she couldn't hold the act and held her lips closed until, her face nearly blue, she blurted, 'What can I do to get it through to you, Voss? This is serious.'

Spittle sprayed onto her hands and my face. I tried to hold my composure because she was right, it was serious, but levity was what I needed right now. She probably did too. I lifted the tissue box and passed it to her. She wiped her face and hands while I took out a handful of tissue and wiped mine. I hadn't expected her to revert to our training days, so I put it down to nerves.

'Voss, Peter Peters is demanding to know who died first. Luke or Estelle?'

I finished her sentence, 'Because if Luke Peter's died first, he left everything to Estelle, but if she died first... I guess he is the sole beneficiary?'

'Jesus, who'd call their kid Peter Peters?'

'I don't know, God obsessed Catholics, or just maybe even they didn't like him at birth.'

'That'd do it.' She was smiling now, but I knew it wouldn't last.

'The bloody parasite, they're not in the ground yet and he wants their money.' I walked around and put a hand on her shoulder. She flicked it off. 'Better put the little Peters man on your suspect list too, Boss, because he's got more to gain from their deaths than me.'

In a flash her demeanour was back to normal. 'Would he have done it though?'

'I don't think so,' my mind went back to the few times I'd met him and the need to wipe off his soft, wet handshake, 'this is too brutal. If pushed, I'd put him down for a poisoner, whoever did this is tough, used to death and Peters is a marshmallow.'

She turned and checked her image reflected in the window. Two manicured fingers pushed a lock of hair back into place. 'Look Voss, you know the Assistant Commissioner despises you and if I don't pull you from the case, he'll demand your suspension anyway. Take some leave, it'll be easier all round.'

'Not for me, but I'll take suspension on full pay. Might give me time to fix my golf swing.'

'You don't play golf.' Her composure was back.

'Well, my garden needs work.'

She stood. 'Look, just stay away. I don't want you doing anything that will compromise the case when it comes to court.'

'You know it might not even come to court unless you find out who killed them and why. Of course you might get a lucky confession, and even if Lucy is the best one on the team, without me, you're still a man down.'

She puffed herself up and straightened her skirt. 'I need your warrant card and gun now,' her hand was out, 'from now on, I'm taking over your role and Lucy will carry on as my number two.'

I thought about saying something smart, but held it in. I tapped the paperwork waiting for attention. 'Want me to sign off on these tonight and Lucy can pick them up on her way to work tomorrow, Ma'am?' I hung onto the last syllables knowing it would grate.

'Grow up Voss. Be at my car in ten minutes.'

'So what is it, suspension or leave?'

'You're suspended until I say otherwise.'

'On full pay...?' I gave her the holster and my card and I turned to lift the papers from my in-tray. 'Should I take these with me? Otherwise you'll need to sign all of these overtime and expense accounts, Ma'am.'

'No bloody way. Jeeze Voss, they should have been processed by now,' she waved her hand over them as if they were excrement, 'take them with you and I'll pick it up in the morning.'

Before she reached Lucy's desk I called out to her, 'About my salary, Ma'am.'

She didn't look back. 'It doesn't change, Voss.'

I smiled at the picture it created in my mind. A caricature of Una Knight stomping off with an Elmer Fudd style storm cloud above her head.

The moment she was out of sight, Lucy came in and sat across from me.

'You okay, Sir?'

'No, I'm pissed off, but probably not as much as you will be.'

I wondered how long it would take for Una to get under Lucy's skin.

'And why's that?'

'She told me she was commandeering this office until I come back,' I held my arms wide to drive home the point, 'and she's welcome to it.'

Her expression changed immediately. 'No way Voss. This isn't happening. How will we get anything done with her hovering all over us? She can't be serious.' She put her head in her hands. A split second later, she looked up. 'What, she thinks she's going to replace you?'

'Yep,' I closed my briefcase and picked up my jacket, 'I have to go.'

Surrendering my car wasn't something I'd counted on. If I was going to find Estelle's killer, I'd need something to get around in. The collection of pursuit cars in my collection, my museum to automotive policing behind my house, were not an option. I needed something more modern. Brett, the manager of the police garage, knew I collected and always kept me informed about anything special coming out of service. He pointed me to a row of decommissioned divvy vans.

'Come on mate, you know I'd never be seen in one of those. What else is there?'

Brett and I had played this dance more than once. I walked to the door and he ushered me outside. Behind the wash bay he had a car cover over something.

'A bloke in accounts bid for this in the last auction. His money was due last week, I've been chasing him ever since, but he phoned yesterday and said to send it back to the sales. Can't raise the cash.'

'Pity,' I said.

We pulled the cover off. 'It's yours if you want it. If not, it's gone. I need your answer now.'

'I forgot you were a car shark on the side.'

'Just doing my bit for the taxpayer.'

I looked at the kilometres, checked the tyres and lifted the bonnet. It was all show. We both knew I was going to take it. We went back to his office and filled out the necessary forms. I gave him a deposit and arranged to come back with a bank cheque the following day.

Una was in her car when I came out of the garage. I opened the back door and dropped my briefcase on the seat.

'Where the hell have you been, Voss?'

'Arranging a car,' I smiled and watched for her expression, 'ex pursuit, low mileage, supercharged Falcon. You'd love it.'

'You're not taking this suspension seriously, are you?'

'More than you think, Ma'am. But are you sure you can solve this without me?'

She turned toward me, her face red. I could see fire in her eyes. 'Don't forget I've been doing this as long as you Voss.'

'Good, you're angry. You'll need to be to solve this one.'

'Oh piss off.'

If I had to suffer suspension, she could do with a bit of extra pressure. She would need to prove to the team that her skills were as good as mine.

We stopped alongside my letterbox. Eddie had the garage door open, he waved.

'Who's that?' She asked.

Before I could answer, her phone rang. She turned away and, lucky for me, held it far enough from her ear for me to hear Lucy's voice. 'Ma'am we have another one, victim shot in a diplomatic vehicle across the road from the Nauru Consulate. Forensics are on the scene. Same M.O. as Adderton, bullet to the head.'

I climbed out, grabbed my briefcase, blew her a kiss and closed the door.

CHAPTER SEVEN

Eddie had changed his mind about working in the garage and my lounge room looked like a big kid's playground. The large flat screen TV I'd shouted myself for Christmas was on the long southern wall and running a spreadsheet. Another television of similar size was to the right of it and another flat-screen of dubious age alongside that. Below them a makeshift shelf, built from sinter bricks and what looked to be two rows of scaffolding planks ran the length of the room. On the north wall several A4 sheets had been taped together declaring this room was now, *Eddie Central*. I imagined it was his attempt at humour. My kitchen table and the one from my outdoor setting were facing the screens, Eddie's laptop on one, and my old upright under the other. The heavy drapes I used to keep light out of my bedroom were now hanging in the front window. I guessed he wanted to stop afternoon light coming in. My head was spinning, trying to take it all in, and I wondered if he'd substituted the ones they'd replaced.

'Like it?' He asked.

'Where'd the other TVs come from?'

Not waiting for an answer and trying to come to terms with the changes, I wandered into my bedroom and found the lounge room drapes hanging at the windows. Back in the lounge room, I stood beside him and scanned everything again, trying to look at every aspect of his control centre. I saw a reflection of his mouth moving in one of the black screens and forced myself to listen.

'Got them at Vinnies. You'd be surprised at what people throw away these days. The TV near the window was left outside their back door last night. They said if I wanted it to come and take it from the footpath. By the time I got there, a bloke was trying to get rid of the other one and a couple of old desktop computers, so I grabbed them as well.'

'Yeah?' I said, and wondered if he had the makings of a hoarder.

He had that mad glint in his eye and rubbed his thumb and forefinger together.

'We worked out a deal,' he paused, as if understanding I needed time to process his words, 'the bloke even delivered them for me.'

I stood there, hands behind my head still trying to come to grips with how quickly my home had become Eddie's headquarters

'Well, what do you think?'

'What do I think? I reckon you've wrecked the place, that's what I think. You can't bring all that old stuff in here,' I waved at his temporary credenza, 'everything belongs down the tip,' I tapped his computer, 'and this table belongs in the kitchen.'

'Settle petal, It's just a house.'

'No, it's not just a house. It's my home and I had it the way I like it. And I don't like it when it's messed up like this.'

'She'll be right. We'll switch it all back when I'm set up in my own place. Anyway, do you want my help or not?'

His attitude seemed way too dismissive, and then it struck me. I knew how he scored the televisions and cash.

'Where's my Whitely?' I was almost shouting.

'What?'

'Where's my Brett Whitely? I pointed to the bank of TVs. 'The painting that was on that wall.'

'In my room, why?'

'Do you know what it's worth?'

'I'm not stupid Voss, it's a Whitely original. I have an old colleague who deals in paintings, I know what it's worth.'

'You didn't tell him, did you?'

'Give it a rest. I just said I wasn't stupid. I thought if we ended up with people coming here, then the Whitely was better off where it wouldn't get damaged.'

'People coming here, are you out of your mind?' My finger was inches from his nose, 'mate, I don't entertain.'

'No, but I do.' He reached for the mouse and started to shut the screens down. I put my briefcase on the outdoor table. I assumed it was for me to use because he looked at home at the other one. Now I'd acclimatised to my lounge room becoming *Eddie Central*, my senses were swamped by something else. I headed toward the kitchen.

'You'd better clean up,' he said, 'we have company for dinner at seven.'

'Who? You'd better not have invited a bunch of your dero mates.'

'That's a bit harsh, even from you Voss.'

'Then who?'

'No one you don't know. Besides, I need some information to test my algorithms.'

'What algorithms?'

'Look, you want to find out the where, who, why, and when, don't you?'

'Yes.' Then I remembered the job I'd asked him to do. 'What was on the memory stick?'

'All in good time.' A hand waved in front of his face.

I felt my temper rise. He was dismissing me again. Two days ago he'd been living in my front yard and here he was usurping me in my own home. 'No, I want to know now.' I was beginning to regret asking for his help.

'Just some porn and a contact list. Most of it cryptic, but I reckon after our visitors go home I can crack it.'

'Visitors, just who are these bloody visitors?' My life was spiralling beyond my control. This morning I'd had a home and a job, now it seemed I had neither, at least not in the form I'd known them to be.

He tapped his nose and smiled. 'They mightn't even show up, but on the other hand they might. I said it was special occasion, very special.'

'So they're my friends then. '

'Well yes, sneaky yeah?' He was grinning like a kid who'd swiped the last cupcake.

'So you won't say?'

'Nope, because you'd probably try and cancel, but like I said, I need something to finish my programming, and tonight should do it. They won't know they're even helping.'

'Well good luck with that then, because everyone knows I never do social evenings.'

I walked into the dining room and saw the table set for five, then on to the kitchen. I was about to open the oven, when he called out for me to leave it alone. The aroma I'd smelt before when I first arrived home had come from a leg of lamb roasting in the barbeque, and the smell of that, mixed with those coming from some kind of red wine and rosemary reduction simmering on the stovetop, took the edge off my mood.

I took his advice, showered and changed.

At seven I heard cars in the street and three doors close and the clatter of high heels and women's voices, all gossipy, and I recognised each of them. I didn't need this. The last time I'd had a female guest had been so long ago

I couldn't remember it. I was either at work or home alone and since Eddie moved into the garden, the sight of him would have driven anyone away. I tried to shake the thought loose and opened the door to the last three faces I expected to be on my porch tonight. Then it dawned on me, telling them it was a special occasion would have been the only way he could get Una, Gabby and Lucy to agree to this. However, I had no idea what he'd told them.

'Are you just going to stand there with your mouth open, or can we come in?' Lucy looked at me in expectation as I came into the room, 'Can't wait to meet the little woman?'

'Sarcasm does not become you,' I said and called, 'Eddie your guests are here.'

I heard the clink of glasses. 'In here, what are we drinking?'

I ushered them down the passage and into the kitchen where my sofa and armchairs now lined the walls.

'I like to talk to everyone while I'm cooking, don't you?' Eddie said, 'Please sit.' he waved his hand around, motioning to the chairs. To me, his accent was too camp and I wanted to tell him to put a lid on it. He must have heard what I was thinking because he was back to himself with the next sentence.

'Look, I'm sorry, but today's not a special occasion. Eddie has it wrong, but seeing as he's gone to all this trouble, we're glad you could come.'

'I expected... Lucy said, 'well, I don't know quite who I expected, but I guessed a woman.' she sounded confused. 'The note left on my desk said it was from *Voss's partner* and I just assumed.'

I saw Eddie open and close his mouth and was pleased nothing came out.

Gabby put her drink down and faced Lucy. 'When the invitation said his partner,' She did that speech mark thing with her fingers. 'was throwing a surprise dinner, my curiosity got the better of me,' She picked up her glass and pointed at me. 'because I don't know. How long is it since you've been on a date, Voss?'

Her question made the others laugh. I was still pissed off with the situation but, with people in the house and the promise of good food, I let myself fall into the spirit of the evening. Only Una seemed quiet. Eddie must have noticed it too, because he sidled up to her. He had an easy way with women and I was beginning to envy that side of him. He whispered something that made her laugh and I could see her begin to thaw. She only reverted to the Una we knew once, when Lucy said something about the last murder. Her bristles rose, a reminder that any mention of work was off limits for me.

The night had only one more stumble. Eddie had five ramekins of bread and butter pudding on a tray and was setting one in front of Una, when Gabby asked him if he'd always known he was gay. He nearly dropped the tray and puffed up all macho, deepening his voice as if to prove his protests. I thought it was poetic justice for his earlier antics.

Eddie tried to deflect attention to me. 'Soon you'll be telling them about me lodging in your garden and how you took pity on me and conned me into coming inside.' I didn't like where this was headed. What was he thinking? Surely he wasn't going to tell these three what I had asked him to help with. I was speed dialling my brain trying to think of a way to shut him up when he continued, 'Yes, before I had to spend another Canberra winter under the stars. He said you didn't need the grief if I died on his property.' He swivelled his head from side to side and looked at the women with an open mouth that made him look like a carnival clown. 'I mean really?'

'Yeah, there is that.' I said.

'And then I suppose you'll tell them how you're helping me to get back on my feet.'

'I will?'

He slapped the table with his towel and sat down. 'Bugger it Voss, you just did.'

His banter had everyone laughing. He had told part of his life story to strangers without making anyone feel sorry for him. I admired that.

At the end of the night and while they complimented Eddie on his culinary skills, my mind was still trying to process the reason behind this impromptu dinner. Una looked at her watch and made an excuse to leave, the others made similar noises. Eddie asked them for their phone numbers and I watched as he punched them into an iPhone. I wondered whether they had given their private or work number or something fictional as it was hard to imagine them handing out their details to someone so recently homeless. Still, he had shown he could turn on the charm when he wanted to.

'Where'd you get that?' I nodded to the phone in his hand. The one I'd picked up for him was just a basic model.

'Salvos,' he said and winked at me, 'one of my two favourite stores.'

We walked to their cars and I watched as Lucy and Una drove off. Gabby lingered a little longer. I noticed her holding Eddie's hands in hers as she thanked him for a lovely meal. She stretched onto her toes and kissed his cheek goodbye. He held her car door open, not shutting it until the seat belt was on. He stood in the street and watched her drive away.

'Righto, now we've got work to do,' he was all business as he steered me into the kitchen, 'tonight, you do the dishes. I've got things to do in the command centre.'

CHAPTER EIGHT

I threw the tea towel into the laundry hamper, put a fresh one on the rail, opened the fridge and grabbed a couple of beers. Eddie had some explaining to do.

'Righto, Einstein? Are you going to tell me what tonight was all about?'

'What?' He was studying one screen while numbers scrolled down another. Eddie was transfixed. A map of Canberra flashed up on the other screen and three different coloured dots followed the highway. One of the dots broke away and headed toward Deakin. 'Una's going home.' He clapped his hands together. 'Voss old mate, the system works.'

'What do you mean, the system works?'

'I've duplicated the same app that pizza places use, you know, when you can track the driver who delivers your order. By putting in a date and time, I can even see where Ms Knight was yesterday. Here I'll show you.' He clicked on the dot and Una's name and phone number followed the dot on the screen, a drop-box asked for the date and he filled it. A purple line traced her movements around Canberra and, once at the work place, it changed colour. 'Now she's walking, see how it's turned to green,'

The green line scribbled back and forth until it made a lopsided dot.

'Great, but how does that help?'

'That doesn't, but if I type in any number from any mobile phone or dongle, it will plot its travel on any day over the last two years.' He was grinning, 'you know, I thought I might've let some of the old brain cells die, but I reckon I can still keep up with today's whiz-kids.'

'And this is good because?'

'You said you wanted to know where and what Luke Peters had been up to, right? Well type in his number and the dates you want to follow him in here,' he moved the cursor to the drop-box while I pulled out my phone and looked for the number.

'Nah,' he waved the suggestion away, 'it's in the system.' That bloody flash of colour coming from those dancing eyebrows and grin of his were working overtime. I knew he was enjoying winding me up.

'How?' I said.

'Easy. I hacked into your phone contacts while you were in the shower.'

'You went through my pockets?'

'Didn't have to, your Bluetooth was switched on and I downloaded from there. Same as I did with Una, Lucy and Gabby, who is rather nice by the way.'

'Probably reminds you of your daughter.'

'She does a bit,' he turned back to the screen, 'that's why I like her.'

Satisfied Eddie was on track, I opened my briefcase and I started signing off on the expense and wage claims. I grabbed the data logger as it rolled to the back of the case. 'Here this is for you.' I threw it across the tables.

'What is it?"

'The data logger from the crashed BMW.'

'Oh good,' his fingers moved like those of Fagin in the Dicken's films, 'and do we have an interface?'

'What's an interface?'

'The bit it plugs into. Or a scan tool?'

It sounded like gibberish to me, but tech stuff always had. I finished the claims and left them on the desk. 'I'm off to bed. Una will be here before eight to collect this lot.'

'I could always stop her car.'

'What?'

'You know, hack the manufacturer's system and put in a fault.'

'You can do that?'

'Easy.'

'No. Don't touch it.' I stressed the point as I left the room, bidding him goodnight as I went.

I slept better than expected. Considering all that had happened in a short space of time. When Eddie, dressed in matching Adidas tracksuit and shoes came through the front door, I was making breakfast.

'Don't tell me, Vinnies?' I asked.

His hands were on his knees, 'Salvos this time.' He was sucking air like a giant grouper, when he looked up the smile of his was infectious. 'Got to give it to Canberra, they throw away some good stuff.'

'Why didn't you do this before?'

'Do what?'

'Clean yourself up. I've been saying for ages you should come inside and start living again. See what you've been missing?'

'We'll see how well I do first, eh.' He slapped me on the shoulder and looked toward the screen with Canberra on it. 'She'll be here in five minutes, Voss.' He closed the door.

I was in the street when Una arrived and other than a nod as I slid into the seat, it was as if I wasn't there. She remained silent, even after I'd asked her to drop me at the bank so I could pick up a cheque I'd organised to pay for the car. However, the silence must have been getting to her.

'So what's the deal?' She said.

'What do you mean?'

'Well you often said you had someone living in your garden, but I always thought you meant a garden gnome or something. And now we get to meet him who, by the way, has a great touch in the kitchen,' I heard a question in her voice but didn't see the need to enlighten her, 'but he doesn't look like any homeless person I've come across on Northbourne Avenue.'

I was tempted to elaborate, but decided to add similar pressure to the stuff she'd often put on me. 'So, what are you doing to prove the killer isn't me?'

'I can't discuss the case with you Voss, any more than you could if our roles were reversed.'

'You can prove I didn't kill the last one, so tell me about that.'

'Shit, Voss. What do you want me to do?'

'Find the bloody killer or killers. Think about it. There had to have been more than one killer at the Peters' place. I know forensics are swamped at the moment, but they must have something by now. Ma'am, this is important. My career's at stake here. Eliminate me as the murderer and go from there. Luke Peters had heaps of clients who were more than capable of doing it. I set the team interviewing the bit players. Lucy and I were going to start working through the organised crime bosses but, as the body count built, our resources were stretched. Take some muscle and start with the big bosses first would be my advice.' I had another suggestion, but held it in.

'I can run your team, at least until you get back.'

'So, what can you tell me about last night's victim?'

'Oh, give it up Voss, take Eddie on a holiday.'

She pulled up in front of the bank. I handed her the wage and expense forms and went on my way.

Glad to be away from her I entered the bank and picked up the cheque. By eleven o'clock, my mission was complete. I received a call from Una asking me to return my work phone. I had thought about leaving it at the desk, but took the opportunity to find out how the team's briefing went.

'Out, Voss.' Lucy spotted me and nodded toward to my office where Una was on the phone. 'She's trying to find more resources. You should be happy, apparently you're so difficult to replace, she's trying to add three senior officers to the team.'

'Well that is flattering. I'll bet they'll be part of my budget when all of this is over.'

'Come on, you know you can't be in here.' Taking me by the arm, she started to usher me out of the room when I faked tripping over. Bending down to retie my shoe lace I kept my eyes on the evidence board. Having memorised the last victim's name and the car owner, a hire company, *Canberra Limousines*, I had another lead. Once clear of the building, I scribbled down the victim's name, the plate number of the limo and the location of the shooting.

After taking delivery of my new car, it was time to purchase a phone. I knew others in the force had their personal mobiles, but I hadn't needed one until now. Driving home I felt the rush of power underfoot and smiled to myself, all I had to do next was to get Eddie to talk to someone about hiring a limo.

CHAPTER NINE

I was desperate to get to the hire company, but Eddie insisted we stop in at Cash Converters first. I hated the place and it made my skin crawl, with its shelves heavy with the misfortunes of others. From the moment I could afford nice things I tried not to buy anything that had a previous owner. My only exceptions were if it was an investment opportunity like the Whitely, which came from an unexpected inheritance not long after Estelle walked out the door. A compensation for not having kids, a woman once told me. Eddie however, was in his element, carrying a shopping basket filled with a mad scientist's spaghetti of coloured cables and electronic fittings.

He stopped at a glass cabinet. 'Scan tool,' he said and pointed. The sales assistant passed it to him. 'I'm looking for a photocopier too, or a printer that will take A3 sheets.'

The counter jockey shook his head and suggested we try the copier place or recyclers further down the shopping strip. We walked past a box where a staff member was throwing out old model smartphones.

Eddie stopped and rifled through them, 'I'll give you ten bucks for a dozen of them,' he said to the assistant.

'Can't, they're going off to be recycled.'

'Could you ask your boss for me, please?' He laboured the please.

A moment later a nameplate almost big enough to hide the woman wearing it was standing in front of him. 'How can I help?' She asked.

Eddie's voice changed to a sing-song tone as he addressed her. 'I see that all these phones are going off to the crusher and wondered if you could help me out? I work with underprivileged people, re-training those who have found themselves out of work and wanting to get on their feet again. Teaching them about electronics and current technology helps with that.' He clasped his hands and looked skyward. Madam, if you could see your way to letting me have some of these old phones, it would be an enormous help.'

The sugar in his voice made it hard for me to keep a straight face, so I sauntered over to the jewellery cases. I could still hear him, but I was sure no-one would see my expression. The saccharine approach worked his magic and the manager allowed him to choose ten phones. He asked if he could take the chargers too. I heard her sigh and say, 'take what you need,' I could feel the exasperation in her words, 'you can have this lot on the house.'

'Bless you,' he said, beckoning to me as he walked her to the check-out.

As I tapped my credit card's security code into the screen, I thought about Eddie's love of technology and how it could become a point of frustration if I let it continue.

He loaded his bag of goodies onto the back seat. 'Recyclers next, I need material to build a frame and then to the hardware for brackets and stuff.'

'Hold your horses, is this for you or me? What the hell do you want a photocopier for?'

'Parts, Voss, parts. I talked to a young bloke from the Uni today and he gave me a list of what I need to assemble the necessary hardware.'

'What hardware?'

'Crime fighting technology. It's what you asked me to do and you're going to love it.'

'Look mate, all I want to do now is to solve a murder and clear my name, not fill the house with junk.' I didn't look at him, but I knew he was grinning. 'That's why I asked for help.'

'Yeah and I'm helping, you just have to wait a while until I get this sorted. A tradesman's only as good as his tools, you know. The sooner I'm set up, the sooner we'll find your killer.'

'You make it sound so easy. Almost like I know nothing and you can find the person or persons just like that.' I snapped my fingers to emphasis my point. He was beginning to get under my skin, an itch of my own creation 'I've been catching the bad guys for over twenty-five years without much more than my intelligence and skill.'

'Not doubting it. Some of it luck, and some detective work I imagine,' he paused for effect, 'let's eliminate the luck side though, shall we?'

I wanted to rebuke him, but thought better of it. 'Is there anything you haven't thought of while we're traipsing around?'

He was looking at the scan-tool. 'I need to find a car wrecker and buy an interface.'

'Before, or after we go to the limo joint?'

He tapped the screen on his phone and directed me to an address in Fyshwick. It wasn't far from the limo company, or the film set warehouse so I was happy to humour him.

Twenty minutes later we stopped in the recycler's carpark and Eddie sauntered into a shed that seemed to serve as an office.

Left to my own thoughts, I wondered why Estelle would add me to her will. I picked up Eddie's phone and rang her mother. She asked about the investigation, I told her what I knew and how uncovering Estelle's new will had me removed from the case. She accepted my re-assurance that the team would catch the killers without me. I asked her if she had any idea about Luke Peter's dealings, or if she had thought of anything more that might point the team to where to start looking for clues. She couldn't. I did learn the funeral time though and thought about another expense, Eddie would need a suit.

Looking like a kid with a show bag, Eddie opened the door and slung his goodies onto the back seat. 'Now for the photocopier. It's just up the road, a place that sells second-hand units has a pile out the back ready for the crusher. Just what we need.'

'And the limo company?'

'Yeah, yeah, but first things first. These blokes knock off early. Hire car joints are always open.'

He had a point. I backed out and followed his pointing finger as he craned forward scanning the verges.

'Whoa stop.'

I hit the brakes and pulled over. 'What?'

'There in the grass. Be back in a jiff.' He was out the door and rummaging around in front of a half burnt out car. He was back with more stuff. 'Pop the boot,' he yelled, 'this stuff's a bit grubby.'

'What is that?'

'Fuse box trip computer, odds and sods.' He was grinning again, 'right price though.'

'Larceny through finding is still a crime.'

'Nah, public service. Cleaning the street up.'

His phone rang and he listened for a while before putting it in the console, then he was pointing again. 'Two blocks on the right, park out the front and they'll bring it out on a trolley for us.'

'Bring what out?'

'Auto-feed, collating copier. Probably needs a drum and toners. They said the glass is good, no scratches, but because it's old and has a printing problem, they're junking it. That won't bother us though, and the price is right. They told me to come back if I want any more.'

'We won't, will we?' I could see my home fast filling with junk.

'Have to see if everything works. Now to get another Sim card.'

'No way mate. Right now, you're going to get some info for me.'

The limo company was in the same industrial estate as the film set. I studied each factory this time. A patrol car was parked out the front and I recognised it as one allocated to my team. A plainclothes officer walked towards it, phone to his ear. I wanted to walk over and listen in, but resisted the urge.

Eddie opened his door, bent down and waited for my instruction. 'Just go in and ask about their service, drop Luke Peter's name,' I said, 'I'll wait out here. Check the number and style of the cars. Then tell them you're an insurance broker and ask if you can quote them.'

'Yeah, yeah, easy. Leave it to me.'

I looked at him and thought he'd started to enjoy the roleplay. 'Go,' I said, 'these coppers don't know you.'

He looked more Microsoft geek than insurance broker, but I was confident he'd schmooze to get the information.

I got out of the car and walked around the block of buildings, taking care to stay out of sight of anyone who might identify me. Everything was uniform in this group of factories, on one corner I understood why, they'd all been built by the same company. A stone edifice declared this to be a Milano Developments Project, a Peter Peters company. Finally, I had a connection. Peters, or someone from his company, had information we needed and I hoped the hacking skills of my houseguest would save a confrontation.

The police car had gone by the time I got back to mine, but overhead a police chopper swept in ever decreasing arcs across the sky. Probably nothing to do with this case, but natural curiosity had me questioning its presence. As it dipped below the roofline of the building, I noticed every inch of the place was covered by security cameras. The nearest was attached to a light pole close to where we'd parked. I grabbed my camera and zoomed in getting a clear shot of its serial number. I didn't fully understand exactly what it was Eddie did, but thought he may be able to use the information.

I didn't have to wonder long, as he walked up and stood beside me. He leaned in to look at the screen on the camera and said, 'you wondering, what I'm wondering, Sam?'

'Could be. What are you wondering?'

'Who's watching who?'

'That's what I'm thinking, too.'

'I reckon it's strange, because there's no security company decal on anything here.' He scratched his temple. 'Companies who do this stuff usually can't wait to put their name on everything.'

'I'll ask,' I said and shrugged. 'what can they do, arrest me?'

'I'll show you another way, a quicker cleaner way. It might just take me a while, that's all.'

'That's okay, but for now, I'm going in.'

It took a minute for my eyes to adjust, the warehouse was dark and the empty office was nothing special. A couple of plastic pot plants at the end of the room had once added a touch of style, now they reduced the space to cheap kitsch. I could see people washing cars and, to the side, there appeared to be a driver's room. I wandered across and announced my presence to a bloke in a chauffer's suit, his collar undone and tie loose.

'Who's the boss?' I asked.

'Not me, but what can I do for you?'

'A couple of my colleagues were in here earlier, but they forgot to ask how much work you did for Luke Peters? Can you help us with that?'

'He only used us if he was going somewhere special. His wife ran the business,' he looked up as if to trying to compose himself, 'pity about her death, she treated us good, but I'd still like to know what happens now with the new owners.'

'You have new owners already? How do I get in touch with them?'

'Well, Peter Peters reckons it's him, but I guess he'll have to wait until it's formalised, like the rest of us, I suppose.'

'Thanks'

Eddie was half in, half out the car fiddling with his iPad when I got back. I closed the door and reached for my seatbelt.

'Everything to do with security is linked by Wi-Fi,' he said, 'I told you it was easy.'

I wondered if I should ask how he'd bypassed the firewalls, but decided it was better not to know. 'Ready?'

'Sure, home James.' He pulled his feet in and closed the door without taking his eyes from the screen.

The touch screen in the car beeped. 'What's that?'

'And Houston, we have a picture.' Suddenly his accent was Texan.

'See, that's us.' I looked at the screen and thought the car looked better in real life.

'Bloody amazing what this stuff can do,' he looked at me, his grin made his eyes glow like blue and green LEDs, 'but now we need more SIM cards.'

'Not yet. I need a chat with Estelle's solicitor, and you're going home.'

'That'll work too,' he said.

I hated visiting solicitors at the best of times. I didn't have any time for them and I had even less trust. When Estelle and I divorced, it felt as if I'd gone in through a revolving door with my lawyer. He came out in my new suit with pockets full of cash and me? I was penniless and naked.

CHAPTER TEN

Eddie went straight to the laptop when we arrived home.

'Before you sit down,' he said, 'I'll need you to help me with that copier and what do you have in the way of tools?'

He tapped a few keys and coloured lights danced across his map of Canberra. It reminded me of watching the train network I'd seen in a control room when I was a kid.

'Where's Lucy right now?' I asked.

He clicked her name in a drop box and the address came up. 'At work,' he said.

'I can see that.' It annoyed me when people stated what I could see for myself.

'Keep your shirt on. You want to know if Estelle's solicitor is in?'

'Yeah,' I scribbled down the number, but he'd loaded the data in my new phone already. 'Smart-arse. How did you do that?'

'I copied all of Estelle's contacts from her phone. He was in it.'

'But we didn't find her phone.'

'We didn't need to. Once I had her number and a couple of others that I guessed were in her address book, I hacked it.'

'That's not legal.'

'No, but you've got to admit it is clever.'

'So find me something I can use. Find me the people who wanted Luke Peters dead.'

'Look it's good, but it's not a time machine.' He scratched his head for a second and rummaged through his treasures from Cash Converters. 'You've given me an idea though. Go see Estelle's solicitor. Check up on your inheritance.'

I slapped the table where he was working, 'come on, you can help me get the stuff out of the boot first.'

'Yeah, yeah,' he waved at me, 'in a minute.' He shoved a piece of paper at me, 'call into the electronics place, pick this stuff up and organise three more SIM cards too. I'll increase the data allowance once they're registered.'

I took the list. 'You were cheaper to keep when you only ate pizza and drank my beer.'

'Yeah, but we're having more fun now though, right?' That bloody grin again, I wish I'd never told him to smile more. 'Here, and keep your phone on, I might need you to pick up more stuff.'

I slipped it in my pocket.

The solicitor looked exactly as I'd imagined, late sixties, carrying a bit more weight than was healthy, greying hair fading to white around the temples. Although his hands were soft, his grip was firm. I thought of him as fatherly and when he spoke I could tell why Estelle had chosen him. He spoke like a man of trust.

'Thanks for giving me time at such short notice,' I said.

He waved away the suggestion that I might be inconveniencing him. 'I was expecting you before this. Poor Estelle, and is it true what the papers said about her death?'

I turned my palms up and shrugged, he could make of the newspaper reports what he wanted. 'I wondered about her will and when she made it. My team said I was mentioned in it.'

'You and her mother are joint beneficiaries, but there is something else,' he handed me a sealed package. 'I'm not supposed to pass it to you until after her funeral, but under the circumstances...'

'I understand.' I went to slide a finger under the flap. 'Have you seen inside it?' I waved the envelope without looking inside.

'No, and her instructions were to tell you not to read it until you were home.

'That sounds like Estelle,' I folded it in half and worked it into the inner pocket of my jacket, 'but why would she leave anything to me? Other than a few legal functions, I haven't seen her for years. The last time was probably over seven years ago.'

'She knew you were close to her mother. They had no family and she didn't want Luke's brother and his grasping wife, her words not mine, wasting it.' He rolled a pen between his fingers on both hands. 'You know Peter Peters is pushing for time of death.'

I nodded.

'If he challenges the will, what will you do?'

'I'll worry about it when the time comes.' I knew Eddie was working on Luke's assets and overall financial position, but I asked him about Estelle's position also.

'She was pretty much the brains behind the wealth. Luke had the profile, but Estelle had the smarts. She also knew whose palms to grease, moved in when prices were low and sold at the top of the market. Typical entrepreneurial moves. Shifted money off shore and minimised her taxes. She left a fortune. You're a wealthy man Mr Voss.'

'Let's not get ahead of the game yet, we have her murder to solve first.' I wanted to know if he had any notion of why Peter was so desperate. 'Did you do Luke Peter's will too?'

'No, after their divorce, he used a flash mob in the city. I don't think he knew about Estelle's change of will.'

'Divorce! But I thought...'

'Everyone does. They still owned the house together and a few other minor investments, but Estelle pushed for a divorce not that long after they were married.'

'Do you have a list of their current joint assets?'

'I'll get it for you.'

I expected him to call a secretary to find and photocopy it for me but he reached for a folder on his desk instead. 'I thought you might ask, so here's one I prepared earlier.' He laughed at his own joke. 'You'll find who did this, won't you? Estelle was everything her brother in law isn't. Likeable.'

'Thanks for your help,' I said.

He walked me to the door and opened it. His voice softened as we shook hands, 'she was no-one's angel, but murdering her isn't right. Don't be too disappointed in what you find.'

In my car I opened the envelope from Estelle. It had been addressed in her own hand, all copperplate and swirls. I tipped the contents onto the passenger seat. A key and a few loose photos fell out. Most were of us in better times and one from our honeymoon in Port Fairy. I held the key up to the light. I'd seen three like it before. I shoved it into my pocket and the photos back into the envelope. The letter started with, *I'm sorry,* that was enough for me. I folded it and never wanting to read or hear her apologies again shoved it in with the photos. I'd lived with that crap for too long.

The list of assets was illuminating, they shared a few rental properties, but Estelle owned a management company outright. I found this strange, as until now, I'd thought it would be Luke who'd have secret investments, not her. It was time to find out just how independent Estelle had become. Among the solicitor's papers, I found the address of her accountant and decided to pay them a visit.

The phone in my pocket rang, Eddie again. 'I'm going to e-mail you a list of stuff to pick up from the electronics place and Bunnings. Don't worry about the list I gave you, they are picking it now. Just check it off when you pay for it.'

'Hang on, what are you buying and how much.' This was getting out of hand.

'Look I've got to go. Hot date.'

'Who?'

'Someone you know. I'll tell you about it while you help me finish your time machine. Oh, and your boss wants you to call her, something about Luke Peters' brother. Don't forget Bunnings.'

I felt like a puppet with Eddie holding half my strings in one hand and Una Knight holding the other half. I had to refocus quickly if I was to solve this case. The accountant was out of town for a couple of days and would call me when she got back. I ran Eddie's errands with reluctance and headed home.

CHAPTER ELEVEN

Eddie was in his command centre when I arrived home. I slung the bag of electronics at him, before noticing he was a more spruced up version than the one I'd dropped at home earlier. I looked at him and held my hands out in question.

'I told you, hot date tonight. Remember? I'm having dinner with Gabby.'

Once he'd left I settled into having the place to myself and it didn't take long to realise how much I liked being on my own. I looked in the fridge, thought about the left over pasta from the previous night and decided I wasn't hungry. My appetite was for work and from what I'd gleaned from a chat with Gabby when she'd called for Eddie, the team still hadn't located the bloke whose job it was to check the film set after the alarm went off. It bothered me.

In my lounge room, that now looked more like a NASA control module, I googled the address and cross referenced it with Luke Peters' assets. I found nothing I didn't know already and decided that if this case was ever going to move forward, it was time to meet the bloke with the snake tattoo

Technically, I'd inherited part or all of the factory precinct and having a key meant getting in was no problem. However, wanting to know the identity of the Mercedes' driver and his passenger. A plan started to form in my mind.

A drive past showed that most of the companies based here had closed for the day. I parked a block away, pulled a baseball cap down to hide my eyes and slid my arms into a hoodie. I tugged the zipper all the way up and made sure the collar covered the lower part of my face. Now I was ready to play the part of burglar. I grabbed my tool bag from the back seat, secured the car and strolled around the block to the film set. I tried the door but it was locked. I knew the security cameras would have it covered from more than one direction, so I propped a jemmy bar against the wall and set a hammer beside it. Thinking that a walk around the back of the building would reinforce the impression of a thief checking the place out, I spent ten minutes setting the scene.

Back at the door I picked up the hammer. I needed to do something for effect and thought smashing the lock would do. However, I decided if I was a bit clever, I could use the key from Estelle's letter. Changing tools, I pretended to work the jemmy into the gap between the door and the jamb. Careful not to be seen by any of the cameras while I worked the bar with my left hand, I hid the key in my right and inserted it into the lock. A push on the bar and a twist of the key had the door open. I dropped the jemmy and two steps inside, the alarm sounded. All I had to do now was stroll into the bowels of the building and wait.

Within a few minutes, security guard Brad arrived and from the shadows I watched him punch in the code to turn off the alarm. I could hear him report in and say he'd wait. I dialled Lucy telling her where I was and what I was doing. I could hear her car starting before we'd finished the call.

I found a room at the back of the building opposite that gave me a clear vision of the activity and waited for the Mercedes to pull up. I hoped Lucy would arrive before

I needed to defend myself. My fighting skills weren't as good as they'd once been, I was more brain than brawn these days.

A flash of silver whizzed past the doorway followed by the sound of two car doors closing. I heard Brad's voice and strained to hear him. He sounded timid as he explained turning off the alarm and waiting at the door. A figure walked past, a flash of light reflected from my jemmy bar. Holding it in his right hand he slapped it against his left, making me wish I'd re-thought this part of my plan. Feeling around for anything that might be useful as a weapon, my fingers brushed a rectangular metal object and I grabbed at it. As the two figures made their way further inside, I threw whatever it was into the far corner of the room before edging my way out to my right. When I heard them race toward the noise, I ran on tip-toes toward the front door.

Brad had his back against the door jamb. I opened and closed my wallet, hoping he'd think I'd flashed my police I.D. and ushered him outside. Pulling the doors shut behind us, I forced the handle of my hammer between the loops on the door pulls.

'Got them now,' I said, walking him to his van where I pulled the microphone out of his radio and took his keys. 'just sit there until the cavalry comes.'

I made a note of the Mercedes' registration number. It was unlocked, but they'd been smart enough to take the keys out of the ignition. I pulled a pair of evidence gloves from my pocket and slipped them on. Reaching under the dash I opened the fuse panel and found the data logger. After removing it I dropped it into an evidence bag and closed the panel. A quick search of the car turned up a magazine full of bullets, scales and a quantity of deal bags containing what looked like cocaine. I popped the trunk and lifted the floor mat, finding more gear the drug squad would be interested in before using my phone to photograph the evidence.

As I closed the trunk, I could see the blur of flashing lights from Lucy's car and in the distance, sirens warned other units were on their way. Her timing was perfect, I ran back to the door and pulled the hammer away. I was to the left and partially hidden as Peters and Snake Tattoo, like angry ants leaving their nest, burst through. Snake held a pistol in his right hand and as I smashed the hammer down on his wrist it slew across the steps. I hooked it with my foot dragging it behind me.

'Peter Peters. It has been a while?' I said, sounding too much like a line from a bad script, before adding. 'Who's your friend?'

Before he could answer, the tyres on Lucy's car squealed in protest as it wheeled into the carpark. She was out of the car and sprinting toward us as two patrol units filed in alongside.

'Voss, get yourself over there,' she reached down and using a ball point pen in the trigger guard, picked up the pistol, passing it into the gloved hand of her number two. She looked at me and pointed in the direction of her car, 'I'll get to you later.'

I stopped before I got there and leaning on the driver's door of Brad's van, pointed to Lucy who was busy with Peters and his friend. I slipped the keys back into his ignition. 'Thought you said you didn't know these blokes?' I pointed to Peters and Snakehead, 'said you didn't have a number for them the other night and yet when you get here today, you know their names. I hope you've got a good excuse lined up for the Detective Sergeant. She's leading this case now and has five murders to pin on someone. Will that someone be you, Brad?'

He dropped his half eaten sandwich into his lap and I watched his face darken. His chewing stopped and I heard him begin to choke on it. A moment later he coughed and blew chewed bread, chopped lettuce and tomato all over the dashboard. He was reaching for his water bottle when I dropped the radio's microphone at his feet and stepped away. I strolled around the back of Lucy's car, opened the front passenger door and climbed in.

I knew she'd be peeved when she finally got around to talking to me, but there was nothing I could do about it. I wanted to hear everything Peters' and Snake were saying to her, so I lay the seat back, crossed my hands behind my head, closed my eyes and listened. However, the sound of another car caught my attention and I sat forward to see a dark grey limo cruising the block. I guessed the driver had seen the police cars, because he needed to complete a three point turn to ease back along the road. I scrawled its registration number onto the palm of my hand and allowed myself a smile. Eddie would have plenty to do tonight.

CHAPTER TWELVE

It was still light and Lucy was walking toward the car. I assumed that everyone's statements had been taken, and it was time for her to get around to me. There was nowhere for me to go and I watched her through the slits of my eyes. The force of her hand on the door handle shook the vehicle and the door groaned its objection as it hit the stops.

'What are you playing at, Voss? Una told you to stay away and yet here you are playing a bloody burglar. Anyone with sense would have waited until after dark.'

'I...'

'No, you don't.' She held her hand up and I decided not to interject. 'You wanted this, didn't you? You wanted to find the guy with the snake tattoo and I'll give you that, you've found him. I know his name, where he lives, and what he does, but the thing is, I can't share it with you. Won't share it with you, because you and I both know you'll storm in and mess up my investigation. Peter Peters is demanding your arrest for breaking in and false imprisonment. Says he's going to raise hell with the Assistant Commissioner.'

I held up the key. 'It appears that I wasn't breaking in after all.'

'Jesus Voss, did you swipe that from the evidence file?' She grabbed for it, but was too slow.

'Nope, it's mine. Estelle's solicitor passed it over along with some photos and other personal stuff.'

'Why though?'

'Why what?'

'Why go to all this trouble to flush out the snakehead and Peters.'

'Well I saw your board, earlier. You've got nothing. Now you can find out what Luke Peters was up to here. It gives you a lead at least. And I'd take a look in their car too if I was you.'

'Why?'

'Why not, you never know what you might find.'

She called a constable over and directed him to the car. I knew calls to their solicitors would have them bailed in a moment, but it wouldn't hurt to put a bit of pressure back on Peters.

'Wake up, Voss. Luke Peters had nothing to do with this complex. It's in his wife's name, so whatever got them killed might have been about her. Ever consider that?' Her eyes were bulging and the veins on her neck stood proud.

She sprayed the words at me and some of them struck home, but there was no way Estelle was behind any of this. Not the woman I knew anyway. 'Nah, this is all Slippery. He just put stuff in his wife's name to beat the tax man.'

'Sorry, but I don't get it. Even after ten years you're still so in love with her, you'll forgive her anything. Estelle wasn't perfect and she cheated on you. The woman is, sorry, was a witch. You have to let her go, Voss. Otherwise you'll never get over her.' She looked down as if to hide her eyes. 'You've said yourself, probably a hundred times when we've worked similar cases, people make heroes of their dead loved ones. Christ, think about the times you've asked how anyone could compete with a ghost?' She looked at me and turned her palms up.

I said nothing.

'Well, that's what you're doing with Estelle and you know that while it continues, you'll never love another woman again.'

The number of police cars and flashing lights were beginning to draw a crowd. From the corner of my eye, I saw Leonie Smith and her TV News camera crew lurch into the carpark. She was out of the cab and approaching a constable before their van had come to a full stop. He pointed her our way. I raised a finger in her direction, made a 'call me' sign to Lucy, slipped out of her car and walked off. I put my hand in my pocket and rolled the data logger around in my fingers. Got ya!

It was just on dark when I rolled into my garage, Gabby's car was in the street and I could hear her and Eddie in the kitchen. I'm not much of a cook, but by the smell of it, I reckoned he was showing her how to make a bouillabaisse.

'I thought you two were going out.' I said.

'Hello Voss,' Gabby said, 'I have my sister and her new boyfriend staying with me on the weekend and Eddie offered to help me with a couple of recipes. 'There's plenty, you haven't eaten yet have you?'

'No thanks, I want to catch up on a couple of things.'

'Okay, no worries.' She said.

He smiled rubbed his hands together and mouthed the words. 'It's just like having one of the kids around.'

I did my best to ease into the lounge room when Gabby wasn't looking and closed the door behind me. Mesmerised by lights moving over Eddie's map of Canberra, I moved the cursor over one of them and Peter Peters face flashed onto the screen. A list of choices flashed up and I clicked social media to see he had a number of accounts. He'd recently registered on Tinder so I checked his profile, the desperate bastard had posted a photo taken at least fifteen years ago, but that was typical of him.

I typed Luke Peters' name into the search function and a similar list appeared. Maybe Eddie had been doing more than just socialising with my staff. Luke Peters kept many secrets, that was his business, and other than his work details and the occasional cat video, nothing scandalous showed up here. I felt frustrated and decided to concentrate on the bloke with the Snake tattoo. Lucy had called him Andreas, but I didn't know his full name, maybe Eddie's algorithm would turn something up. I entered the Mercedes registration number into the search engine, along with Andreas and snake tattoo. When I clicked on the search icon a split screen appeared on the television to my right. Andreas Raftopolous had lived in Canberra most of his life. I scrolled through the social media files and it was full of soft porn and eBay links. I hovered the cursor over his Centrelink account. His tax file number popped up and that led me into his bank account details, I even found his police record. With that and what Lucy would find on him, he'd find it difficult to post bail.

Peter Peters was a different kind of snake all together and he had enough pull in Canberra to squirm out of anything. I typed his name into the search field again, but this time I looked for partnerships, offshore investments and holding companies, still nothing jumped out at me.

My instincts told me to go back to my training, to follow the money. If Estelle and Luke Peters created the obvious wealth, how did they do it? What companies only generated cash flow and how had he made them look legitimate. I wanted to know which companies were registered offshore, but couldn't find it here. I needed to make sense of the way the Peters brothers hid their money. Who was their banker?

I searched the ASIC website and wrote down every company, the directors and the partnerships, each change of ownership and everything they were involved in. Peter Peters had some less than savoury partners, while Luke Peters was so clean his file smelt like bleach. I was now more frustrated than I'd been an hour ago. Time to rattle the chains of a few Peter Peters' associates.

Ibrahim Damas ran a Lebanese restaurant in the centre of town. He'd been a small-time operator some years ago, then the drug squad ran an operation that cleaned out most of the city's pushers and pimps. After that, Damas had become a bit too affluent to be just a simple souvlaki seller. Tonight, he sat in the back corner of the restaurant while one of his soldiers sat on a stool at the bar with his back to the till. Another sat at a table in the front. To me it looked like they expected trouble, but I wasn't it.

I pulled out a chair and stood waiting until invited to sit. Damas waved and nodded to his staff, a waiter came with a menu.

'Please,' he said, 'we can talk and eat too, yeah?'

'We can,' I took the menu.

'I thought I'd see you sooner than this,' he said, 'and the lovely Una has taken you off the case now.'

I nodded.

'You want to know who's the shooter, eh, and why they're targeting the sophisticates.'

'I'm not sure you'd put Rory Adderton, or the chauffer in the elite category.'

Damas smiled, 'Rory wanted to play there, and the chauffer, he probably saw too much.'

'And Peters, what about him? Why was he killed?'

'I hear it wasn't pretty, must have had some guts to endure that.'

'What do you know?'

'Only what the papers say. No good going after Luke Peters. He was clean.'

'Bullshit.'

'Nothing, the man was straight.'

'What about the brother?' I closed the menu and watched Damas lift a finger to call the waiter. 'Why is he so desperate to pin these murders on me?'

'Little Peters has got big debts due and his creditors are anxious, some are not as patient as me. Always I win,' he closed his menu and we placed our orders, 'I have first call on everything, the banks haven't touched him for years and, let's just say, my lending criteria isn't as strict.'

'How much?'

'Lots, but he's no good to me dead. Alive he keeps borrowing and paying back. When he can't, I get the scraps.'

'That's if the scraps are worth it.'

'They are always worth it, Mr Voss, always.'

We finished our dinner in silence. I started to thank him and say goodbye when Ibrahim raised a finger and motioned me to stay. One of the heavies slid off his stool and stopped a thick set man of islander descent from approaching us. Another of the Damas heavies blocked his path and patted him down.

The Polynesian bowed to my host, 'I have a message from Mr Raftopolous,' he looked at me, 'Mr Voss, Andreas, is a fool., sent back here to get away from his troubles in Sydney. If you can get the police to drop all charges, then Mr Raftopolous will exile him to Greece. Mr Voss, he promises Andreas will be no more trouble for you.'

'How did you find me?'

'I went to your home, your butler said this is where I'd find you.'

'Of course,' I said and looked around for security cameras. Four covered the room, another two covered each till. Ibrahim was not a trusting man, 'I left him a note.'

'Not like you would need to leave a note for Eddie, Mr Voss,' Damas waved a finger at the cameras, 'we all have things we hide and then there are more things we need to see. Your new butler is more than capable of hacking into a security system like mine.'

I turned back to the Polynesian, 'If I can talk to your boss, I'll have a word with Superintendent Knight, but I can't promise anything.'

'We will call you,' he said, before bowing to Damas and turned on his heel and walked out.

'Dwayne will have the number of his car,' Damas said, 'but old man Raftopolous has the penthouse suite at Peppers.'

'And you know this, how?'

'In my business everyone lets their competitors know when they're in town. If they come in without warning, we might see it as aggression and none of us want that.'

'You seem to know what's going on, but you're not giving me anything new. What can you tell me?'

'I can tell you your butler is not called Eddie. I can tell you he is very good at what he does and I can tell you that he too, has money owing to him from unscrupulous borrowers. He didn't deserve to suffer bankruptcy. He should have called those debts in. The price to stand by and do nothing is always too high. I would not have been as generous. That is what Peter Peters worries about, owing money to me.'

I signalled the waiter and asked for the bill. Ibrahim waved him away. 'So, you don't have any theories on who the killer is?' I said.

'No, it has us bothered. We all know who the professionals are and not one of them is in town. The shooter could be military, but I think not. Military would only use one calibre.'

'How do you know more than one gun was used.'

'Eyes and ears, my friend. People see things, people say things and it pays for me to know it. Mine is not a business where you let a competitor have an edge. We are as much in the information business as you are,' he smiled, 'the question you need to ask is, why did they make your pretty ex-wife watch her husband being tortured? Work that out and you have your killer.'

'Gotta go,' I said and stood up.

He walked me half way to the door. 'Estelle played a heavy hand, which is where I'd be looking, if I were you.'

Two of his soldiers slid from their seats and shifted their hands into their jackets, Damas nodded and they stood down.

'Why the sentries?' I asked.

'There's a rogue killer on the loose. We can't be too careful, any of us.'

I thanked him and turned to leave, handing a hundred dollar note to the barman. 'Keep the change,' I said and walked away. It didn't pay to be beholden to anyone in this business.

Parking two blocks from the restaurant gave me time to think as I walked back to the car. Damas had given me the impression he wanted the killer found as much as I did and reckoned this case was all about Estelle, but what could he know that the team hadn't found? Nothing made sense to me. Estelle and her husband had kept their divorce hidden from everyone. I didn't know why and was surprised Damas hadn't tossed that at me.

I stopped to look in a shop window to see if I was being followed, an old habit from my days in undercover. Happy to be alone, I pushed the paranoia aside, why would anyone need to tail me?

I kept running through the concept that Luke Peters had been clean and it was Estelle who had secrets.

If she had amassed this fortune, how had she done it?

Had she had protection from Damas or one of his type, or had it been someone else, someone in authority?

Again, I checked the display in a shop window and listened for footsteps behind me. The Polynesian knowing where I lived spooked me and it set my imagination spinning. My mind had gone into overdrive processing the information Damas had given me. Even Eddie wasn't who I thought he was, something I'd need to sort with him as soon as I got home. By the time I reached the car I was so deep in thought I didn't notice the woman slide into the passenger seat as I got behind the wheel.

'Nice meal?' Una asked.

'You've been tailing me?'

'Let's just say I want to keep you safe. Now you might have eaten, but I could eat a horse.' Her choice of dress was off-duty, but the aura around her was all business.

'Where to?'

'The Boat House. There's a dinner I need to be seen at. We can find a quiet, little corner so it looks as if we're on a date. Don't worry, it's a challenge I've got going with the girls from my tennis club. They think I don't get out enough.'

'Sex and the city?'

'Yeah, something like that.'

Instinct told me there was much more to it than that and I looked at the car parked across the lane from mine. Lucy had the window down and gave me one of those twinkly waves, her gesture telling me she enjoyed the thought of me being stuck between a rock and a hard place.

Una stretched those expensive stockinged legs and smoothed her skirt. I couldn't be sure, but I thought it was for my benefit.

CHAPTER THIRTEEN

As requested. I drove home to change into something Una would accept as fashionable. Parked in my driveway, she remained in her seat and waited for me to open the car door for her. At every turn, I was becoming more irritated, all I wanted to do was solve this case, and everyone seemed to be playing happy holiday.

'Thank you,' she said and held her hand out for me to take as she moved out of the car. 'Now that wasn't so bad, was it? You'll be better at it now you've had some practice.'

Her smile showed she enjoyed this control. I wanted to tell her to find someone other than me to work the crowd at the tennis club, but I knew her motive was less than pure. Una wanted to find out who was in the Peters' social circle, something I wanted to know too. Although I was off the case, I took this to be her way of keeping me in the loop without informing the brass.

'You there, mate?' I called as a warning to Eddie that I was not alone and give him time to close the door on the conglomeration of equipment that was pushing out the walls of my lounge room.

'Yeah, be out in a minute.'

Una walked to a stool at the kitchen island and slid up onto it, poised she waited for me to pour her a drink. The ice seemed to play music as it rattled and cracked when I poured scotch into her glass. She looked around, the smell of fresh cake must have attracted her attention.

'Una,' Eddie appeared from his control room, 'I didn't expect to see you tonight.' I assume he lied, or hadn't seen the car approaching on one of his screens.

'I was lucky to find Voss in the city and convinced him to be my date tonight,' she looked at me, 'now shoo, make yourself look less like a detective and more like my date.'

'So, what, you want me in a tux?' I thought about the last time she'd conned me into one of these things.

'No, I'm not having you do your James Bond routine on me again. Jacket, straight tie and nice pants. If it's not right, Eddie and I will let you know.' She dismissed me and turned to Eddie. 'You've been baking?'

I left the room and wanting to Google search Michael Raftopolous, detoured back to the lounge via the passage. A Sydney crime boss, he had much to hide, but Eddie had a way of discovering the smallest of secrets. I scanned the list, but nothing jumped out at me. It seemed an idea to put his name with Luke Peters. There were a few old cases when they'd been younger, but only the older man had done time on both occasions. I knew it, Luke Peters was a loser.

It was a pain to leave things unfinished, but I needed to squire madam to the ball. After a shower, a shave, and in my best jacket I took a turn in front of the mirror. Nothing would improve my face, but I made the clothes look good. Time to get Una and use the night to prise what information I could from her. She might be using me, but polite conversation always flowed both ways.

'Ready?' I asked and made a gesture toward the door.

She looked me up and down, held her hand out for me to take and slid off the stool, 'You'll do,' she said.

On the way to dinner she grilled me about seeing Damas and my reasons for setting the trap for Peter

Peters and Raftopolous. I could only shrug. I didn't want to let on my secret weapon was a man I'd always known as Eddie. To her and the team he was an upmarket vagrant I'd taken pity on. However, what Ibrahim Damas had told me about him earlier was fighting for reason in my mind. Just what was Eddie hiding and why?

'A penny for them?' she asked. 'What's going on in that suspicious little brain of yours,' she put a finger on my temple,' I can feel those wheels going around.'

For a moment, my mind went back to our uniform days. I always had the case firmly planted at the front of my mind, while Una worked station politics. Times don't change people much. 'You want me to tell you that I had a visit from a Raftopolous heavy and that he had a message from the old man.'

'And the message?'

'You first. Why were you watching Damas?'

'We weren't, but when Gabby phoned to say a heavy from Sydney called at your home. I thought you might need protecting.'

'That's crap and you know it. While I'd love to believe it was your care for me that motivated you, my money's on your need to know what I found out from Damas.'

'Possibly, but just maybe I needed a knight in shining armour to rescue me from the tennis crowd.'

'Come on, there's no way you'd think I'll swallow that.'

'Well Mr Voss, you've seen through my evil plan.'

'Yeah right,' I said and kept my eyes on the road.

'So, what did Damas say?'

'Says the city will be on edge until someone works out who the killer is.'

'And Raftopolous?'

'Wants me to plead for his son's release.'

'So, in your opinion it's not organised crime?'

'I reckon our killer is a rogue from one faction or another. Two options, the first is either a hired gun, or guns who Damas doesn't know, are in town to complete a contract.'

'Yeah, but we'd know. We'd have seen someone fly in. Besides, if the other side say they don't know about it,' she pulled the sunshield down, leant forward and checked her make up. Without looking at me continued, 'so what's two?'

'You first?' I wanted as much from her as she did from me.

'The murder outside the consulate, although it points to a political connection, the killer may have been creating a diversion, or it could be something unrelated altogether.' She flipped the shield back into position.

'So, what does the evidence tell you?'

'No you don't, I'm not falling for that old trick.'

'Everything ties to the Peters' murders. Whatever they got out of Luke Peters was enough to find the others.' I wasn't ready to tell her about the divorce just yet, I wanted to speak with Estelle's mother Donna, first. 'Join the dots, find the connection, then the killer. Simple'

Una faced the window and we rode in silence for a couple of minutes. She spoke first. 'So, your garden ornament, why the charity?'

'Why not? Someone gave me a start once, and right now Eddie can use the leg-up. Nothing more to it than that.'

'Can you trust him?'

I'd played this kind of thing with her before. So, I bit my lip and tried not to get sucked into one of her little mind games. 'You think I'd let him into the house, if I questioned that.'

'He's a fixture then?'

'Only until he gets on his feet. He'll make something happen.'

'A computer geek, Lucy told me.'

'Yep, had me running all over town to get bits and pieces for a project he's had in mind for years. It's too technical for me. I told him to set up in the garage, but he's moved everything into the front room. It needs the air-conditioning or something.'

'Jesus Voss, he could be our killer for all we know. Think about it, he's lived in your side yard for God knows how long, which means he knows a lot more about you than you know about him, and why was he there in the first place? She looked at me for a reaction, 'Look, two people from your past are dead. Who knows, he might have even murdered them out of some sick loyalty to you.'

'Not him.'

'And you are sure of this, how?'

I flicked the indicator on and turned left into the Boat House driveway. 'He was with me at the time of the first two murders.'

'Not him then?'

'Nope.'

'Want me to check his background?'

'Nope.' Although, knowing Una as I did, I was sure she'd already directed someone to look into it.

The Boathouse was decked out in tennis club colours. The men dressed in blazers and slacks, women draped in designer gowns that probably cost as much as a small car. I watched the way soft lighting refracted and danced from pieces of jewellery that hung like flotsam on a sea of spray tanned necks. If you wanted genuine friendship, the tennis crowd would not be the place to look for it, and I wondered why Una bothered with them. Then a couple of political figures caught my eye and I had my answer.

Functions like this had always made me uncomfortable, yet it had been what Estelle lived for. I wanted to leave.

'I know this is a pain in the arse for you,' Una said, 'but humour me, I'll introduce you to a few friends and after you've tended to my needs for half an hour you can go to the bar, or mingle. Your choice, just don't embarrass me.'

A karaoke stage caught my eye and I pointed to it. 'We could do a duet.'

'Don't even think about it.' She led me to the bar and left me there so she could mingle.

I took my drink and moved around the room. It didn't take long to meet people who knew Estelle. Most offered sympathy, but I wondered why most of the men agreed Luke would have been better off without her. This was strange because, on the financial front, everyone said she had the brains. I waited until the speeches were done before joining Brian Fanning, an old colleague of Luke Peters, at the bar. He was sociably lubricated and willing to talk.

'Ruined his chance for the bench by marrying her. The bitch was too ambitious. She cut corners and he was too much of a fool to put his foot down.' The barman put another Crown Lager in front of him and he poured it into his existing glass. 'Gotta break a glass in,' his slur began to tighten its grip on his words, 'I don't know who killed Estelle, but the world's a better place without her and her fucked up schemes.'

'What kind of schemes?'

'You know, the porn parlour, the young girls. Christ some of them hadn't even finished high school when she suckered them in. Once Estelle had her claws into your daughters, she had them for good.'

'Who, Estelle?' I raised my eyebrows, 'when we were together I'd never thought she was as smart as you're suggesting?'

'More cunning than a shithouse rat, that bitch.'

His wife arrived, dressed head to toe Lonsdale Street boutique, and he introduced us. 'Sorry,' she said to me. 'I should have rescued you earlier, Brian runs off at the mouth after a few drinks. I'm Lacey,' she held out her hand, 'nice meeting you, Mr Voss.'

The last I saw of them, his wife was pushing him through the crowd and into a waiting taxi. A few minutes later, she was back in the room, gladhanding women and draping herself over any unaccompanied male. The one man she did avoid, however, was me. Una was doing her own rounds trying to winkle information wherever she could.

I hung around the karaoke stage for a while, the best place to find over-lubricated lips. Pretending to read the song list, I was tempted to take the mike myself and teach Una a lesson but shook the thought off. I wasn't ready to draw any unwanted attention.

With nothing on offer there I spotted Una across the room and she gave me the nod; it was time to leave. I sauntered from the stage and followed her to the car.

'So, what did you learn?' I asked, as I opened the door for her.

'I learnt that you're still the jerk-off you were when we were kids,' she punched my arm as I slid in behind the wheel., 'I saw you chatting up Lacey, and in front of her husband, too. Are there no lengths you won't go to, to feed your ego?'

'Ouch,' I rubbed my arm, 'where does Brian live?'

'Brian who?'

'Brian Fanning.'

'Why?'

'Because he was about to tell me something about Estelle and her business before his wife spirited him away.'

Una pulled the door handle, flicked off her seat belt, and got out of the car so fast I didn't have time to start the engine.

'What are you doing?' I said.

'Come on ladies' man, you have work to do.'

'I'm off the case.'

'Pigs you are. You've got work to do.'

'But I thought you...'

'Change of plan, you chat up Lacey some more and I'll find out why she bundled Brian off home. Give me your keys, and I'll slip out to see Brian. Lacey will be so taken by you she won't even notice I'm gone.'

'How will I get home?'

'Catch a cab, you'll think of something.'

'You owe me.'

'Yeah, yeah,' I could feel her hand in the middle of my back, 'come on, let's get in there.'

The stage was empty and a couple of women were standing by the screen looking at play lists. Lacey was nowhere to be seen.

'He takes requests,' Una smiled at me, 'don't you dear?'

'No, I promised to only sing for you tonight.'

'Pity,' said the woman in a filmy ice blue number that seemed to hide nothing. She ran her hand over my shoulder and down to my buttocks, 'maybe we can tempt you to break the promise.'

A crowd of women gathered in front of the stage while someone braver than I, or who'd had more to drink, sang Misty as Una glided out of the room. Before the song ended, ice blue dress was leaning on me, whispering in my ear. Her breath held enough alcohol to peel paint.

Hoping to spot Lacey in the crowd, I slipped out of her grasp and found a stool at the bar. A couple of tennis jocks muscled in either side of me. They had no idea who I was, but it didn't stop them offering me advice about women, their women.

'What can you tell me about Luke Peters?' I asked, when they'd finished shouldering me back and forth between them.

'He was a womanising prick like you.' Said the bloke with hair that reminded me of a beach when the tide was out. 'Always sniffing around and offering to show the girls how to live a little. Whatever that meant?'

'If you noticed, I neither touched, nor encouraged any of the women in here,' I said.

'Yeah, but you didn't seem to mind another man's wife falling all over you. A man could end up in pieces doing shit like that.'

'So, I can tell the superintendent, you guys sliced up Luke Peters?' I shrugged, 'Murder solved.'

'Piss off. It wasn't us, but whoever it was did us a favour.' His mate, a thick set man with chest hair that tangled through the loops of the heaviest gold chain I'd ever seen added his bit. 'The bastard was a leech, once he got his hooks in, he wouldn't leave a woman alone. I warned him off many a time. It's a wonder he didn't try to bed Una.'

'Probably did, 'said The Beach, 'though she'd be too smart to fall for all his shit.' He passed me his card. He was in real estate.

'What will it be?' They both ordered scotch. I paid the waiter and my two newest best friends gave me a rundown on various members of the club. I wanted to find Lacey, hoping she was primed enough to talk about Estelle.

'Who's the bird who hung all over me before?' I put another note on the bar and the boys had their empty glasses replaced. The waiter put a few coins back on the bar with my other change.

'Oh, that's Patrice, looks hot, feels cold.' Said Beach

'Not when she was talking to me.' I said.

'Careful there. She was one of Estelle's apprentices. Eye on the prize that one.'

Now I understood, Una had brought me here as a divide and conquer ploy.

'Not your cup of tea?' I said.

'I've got a woman who has my balls in her purse and even if she didn't, Patrice would be a price too high to pay,' said Hairy Chain, 'you got a card or something?' He passed me his. He was in Profile Management, whatever that was.

'Thanks, I think I might slink over to Patrice, see how she's doing.' I put a couple of fifties on the bar. 'Order up boys or leave the barman a tip, up to you.' They ordered drinks and Beach counted the change, they had enough for a couple more.

'Thanks,' Profile Management raised his glass to me. I smiled back at him and pushed through the women who were crowding the dance floor.

CHAPTER FOURTEEN

Patrice was nowhere in the room and her friends hadn't seen her for over half an hour. I walked around the deck of the Boathouse looking for Lacey, but there was no sign of her either. Then I spotted Patrice standing at the end of the dock. The lights from the city silhouetted her shape and the filmy material of her gown made her look more Greek Goddess than scheming carnivore. She must have heard my footsteps because she turned and waved at me. As she did, I saw her slip and fall backwards into the water. Shedding my jacket, I ran along the boards, yelling for someone, to call triple zero. My shoes were off and I'd tossed my tie before diving in. I had no idea of how deep it was, so took a belly flop entry into the water.

My hand found something metal, like a shopping trolley. I tried to stand on the bottom and figured the water dropped away to about three metres deep a metre or two from the end of the pier. It was freezing. I tried to recall the image of her leaving the pier. Had she fallen or jumped? From memory it had been almost a liquid movement with no discernible action on her part. I went back to the trolley but found nothing there. Desperate for help, I could hear people above me and I surfaced, yelled something unintelligible and sucked in a large gulp of air before forcing myself back down. The bottom felt as if it was covered in nothing but bags and paper coffee cups. I worked from deep to shallow. There was no current I could feel, but something had to have dragged her away. Air had never been as sweet as that next gulp when I broke the surface. Looking up however, I only saw a crowd of people laughing at me.

Beach reached down to help me out. 'I told you she was a bitch. Patrice is always doing this; she'll be hiding under the dock looking up and laughing at us.'

I slapped his hand away and searched under the dock, there was no sign of her there.

'How well can she swim?' I yelled.'

'About as good as she plays tennis.' That wag's comment brought a roar of laughter from the crowd. 'She can't swim.'

'Come on Patrice, you've had your fun, you can come out now.' One of the wives had the edge of distress in her voice, 'come on girl, your scaring me.'

The dock fell silent.

'Phone the police and ambulance now,' I was shucking off my sodden suit and yelling at the same time,' and tell them we need the dive unit.'

It was critical someone found her soon and it looked like I was the only one willing to get my hair wet.

At four o'clock the divers found her. A bolt from a cross bow had taken out her jugular. Gabby couldn't be sure but thought she would have drowned within moments of hitting the water.

'Christ Voss,' Una pounded up the board walk behind me, 'I leave you to enjoy yourself and you end up in the middle of another murder. Do you do this to piss me off, or is it your way of attracting attention?'

'I gave my statement to Lucy and if it weren't for you I wouldn't be here in the first place.' She offered her hand to help me up. 'I'm going home.'

'I'll get someone to drive you.'

'Just give me my keys and I'm out of here.'

'About your car, well, I had this little ding,' she shrugged to show it was of no concern to her, 'and it was towed.'

'You're kidding me?'

She shook her head and looked away, 'someone will drive you.'

I said nothing on the way home, although the constable continued an attempt at small talk. All I could think was we should now assume anyone close to Estelle, or her husband were targets. Her mother was vulnerable.

I slapped the dashboard, 'turn the car around.'

'What? The Super said to take you home, Sir.'

'Look I know what Superintendent Knight told you, but I'm asking you to go a little out of your way. Estelle Peters' mother is probably a target too. I need to make sure she's okay and take her somewhere safe,' I pointed to the intersection, 'turn right here and I'll direct you. It won't take long.'

'Sirens and lights, Sir.'

'Don't try too hard, Constable, it doesn't become you.'

'I didn't know you played tennis, Sir?'

'I don't. For reasons known only to herself, the super needed a date. Now I find not only did she leave the function, but she's smashed my car too.'

'Sorry Sir, it's just that my mother tried to join that club for years, but every time she had her hopes up, they said her place had been given to someone better credentialed, whatever that meant.'

'It just means they're snobbish and she's better off without them.'

'That's the strange bit, the women were all friends of Mum's.'

'What about your Dad?'

'Sorry, Dad hasn't been around since I was six months old. He bolted, and I've only seen him twice since. Always on the bot. We've been better off without him.'

'So, what did your mum think?'

'Reckons he's a turd.'

'No, I meant about the tennis club women.'

'She sees them as a tank full of piranha, docile and protective until they smell blood. She cut all ties years ago.'

'Good for her,' I said.

We travelled in silence until we reached Donna's address. I went inside and it didn't take much persuading for her to leave with me. She liked life too much to risk leaving it prematurely. I'd called and asked Eddie to make up the spare room and then called Una to let her know the constable she'd assigned to protect me would be with me for a while longer.

Uprooting a woman from her home of twenty years was less difficult that I thought. My ex mother in law had almost fallen in my arms when I asked her to come with me.

'That horrible little man, Luke's brother, and a man with an awful tattoo were here yesterday. He wanted to buy my share of Estelle's estate. Offered me a million dollars for it. Well that's a lot of money to a woman in my position. I told him I'd think about it after I spoke to her lawyer. I phoned him ten minutes later to tell him no deal. He said I might live to regret it. I don't usually swear, but I told him to eff off,' she smiled at me, 'Estelle didn't get her smarts from her father, you know.' She pointed to the suit case.

I picked up the bag, 'Come on, let's get you somewhere safe.' I said and walked her to the car.

Eddie did his best to make Donna comfortable while I showered and changed. Tiredness was going to hit soon and I had a list of things for Eddie to follow up. He and Donna were sharing a pot of tea, a third cup and saucer waited for me.

'You okay mate?' he said as he poured. 'Tea cake? I made it as soon as you said Donna was coming.'

'No thanks,' I brushed the question aside, 'how's your project coming along?'

'Great, but there are some anomalies I want you to look at. Get your head down first, there's nothing urgent.'

'Sure, just don't open the door to anyone we don't know. And see if you can find out when my car will be fixed.' He raised his eyebrows. 'Please?' I drained my tea and went to my room.

I lay there hunting for sleep. I looked at the clock and it seemed to taunt me, challenging me to do something about the case. I rolled images around behind closed eyes. Why did the archer target Patrice? I knew Una would want me to go over the same statement I'd given Lucy, but there was nothing on the night to suspect something like that would happen? The tennis club dinner was one of the types I always avoided. Wives watching the room for any woman who might get too close to their husband, and other women bitching about their men.

The fletching on the bolt from the crossbow would help in identifying the owner and there was no point in me mulling it over. I needed sleep, not questions, so I turned the clock around, it didn't help and these and other questions continued to multiply in my mind.

Why Patrice and what could she have known? Beach and Profile Management had been disparaging about her being Estelle's apprentice. At first, I thought they'd meant her being flirtatious but, with her death, more sinister thoughts rolled and bumped into each other as I tried to force them from my mind. If I had a team I could talk it through with, we could write it on the board and brainstorm to clear the fog. In the end I decided it would be more productive to get out of bed and work rather than count question marks on the ceiling. It was coming on daybreak so I rolled out of bed and showered again.

In the misted mirror over the vanity, I drew faces and wrote names on the fogged-up glass. I discounted Peter Peters but kept him as someone our killer might try to take out next. However, he wasn't exactly keeping a low profile and if someone wanted to kill him it would be easy. Donna had to know more about Estelle than she'd let on. I thought about their relationship. Donna had never approved of Luke Peters but, had still supported her daughter after we broke up. Having nominated Donna and me in her will might be understandable, knowing she'd divorced him. However, it also spoke volumes, Estelle hadn't trusted him.

I wiped the mirror down and got dressed. I could hear familiar voices coming from the kitchen and it dawned on me that it was Lucy and Una questioning Donna. I knew they were probably asking her the same things as I would have, but they were in my home and it made me feel boxed in.

'Don't say anything until I get there,' I called to Donna.

'It's okay,' she laughed, 'we were only talking about you.'

Foregoing a shave, I propped on a stool at the island. Eddie slid a pile of fruit toast and a coffee in front of me.

'Talk to the girls for a bit will you,' he said, 'I've got a few things to do and e-mails to send, okay?'

'Sure, you go.' I watched him close the door to the passage.

'How long have you known Roger?' Donna asked as she watched him close the door.

'Roger, who's Roger?' Lucy asked.

'The man who made you breakfast, Roger Chalmers, remember, he was as big as Dick Smith years ago, then he got caught up investing in some kind of property scam and lost the lot. Most of his friends thought he'd left the country, or died, or something. Had a suite of offices alongside those George and I had once. Lovely man. Anyway, these two friends of yours were asking me about Estelle.'

'I want to sit in, if that's okay?'

'Voss,' Una looked at me with that angry school ma'am look she used on her subordinates, 'you don't want us to do this at the station, do you?'

'I'll be fine, Sam,' Donna's face was deadpan and innocent, 'Estelle kept that side of her life hidden from me, anyway.'

'Go and help Eddie,' Una said, 'do what boys do with old computers and things.'

Eddie was writing code. The sound of a fan whirring came from the machine he'd cobbled together out of mobile phones and the photocopier. Sheets of paper dropped from the printer into the copier feed tray and from there into the different racks of the collator.

'Hey,' I wanted to press him about hiding his identity but decided to do it after Lucy and Una had left.

'Another few minutes, mate and I'll be with you.'

My front room clicked, buzzed and flashed with coloured lights. I pulled a chair out and started to turn on the computer at my station.

'Sorry Sam, the server's busy at the moment. I'll let you know when it's clear.'

I did my best Schwarzenegger impression of I'll be back and left the room.

Donna seemed to be holding her own as I walked through the kitchen. There was no place for me in my own home so I headed down the back yard to the shed where I garaged my car collection. Opening the side door, I looked at the 1969 Mini Cooper S pursuit car. Not a vehicle you would drive every day, but it was a car you'd be noticed in and right now I felt the need to be noticed.

After I'd bought it from another collector, I had to find a few of the chrome mouldings to replace those that had been damaged, but overall the panel work was the same as when it had been in service. I knew the battery would be low on charge so attached a jump-starter, turned the key and waited until the clacking of the dual SU petrol pumps stopped. I drew out the choke and cranked her over. Thirty seconds later, that rorty sound that can only come from a high performance, twelve seventy-five cubic centimetre, BMC engine, filled my man cave. Not wanting to gas myself I opened the roller doors and eased it out onto the courtyard.

My cars were always housed under cover, but the windows needed a proper clean and as I fetched the Windex from the utility shelf inside the door, my thoughts turned to the Peters brothers. Luke Peters always made the headlines, even when he lost a case his profile was in the press. When he won, he made the most of television opportunities, appearing on several morning shows when he'd had a famous television and radio star acquitted of breaching contempt of court laws. His brother Peter had made do with getting his face on air through commercials. Their fraternal dynamic was one of competitive spirit, but I always thought they'd worked together on some of the less reputable schemes. Sure, it was Estelle's name on the paperwork, but I was convinced her husband's money paid the piper. What other reason could she have for sharing a house with him?

Lost in my thoughts I didn't hear Donna come up behind me. 'Eddie's finished with the computer now, says you can use it whenever.'

'You called him Roger before, now you're saying Eddie. I don't understand. I wanted to ask him, but with Una and Lucy...'

'You didn't want to embarrass him.'

'Yeah, I guess.'

'George and I nicknamed him Eddie, he was always talking about taking his business to the stock market, setting up franchises and the like. Well that was the plan until Craig did the dirty on him.'

'Craig?'

'His partner, Craig left his wife and shot through with their secretary, but not before they'd drained the business of cash. Eddie went bust in spectacular fashion. You might remember it was all over the papers at the time. Anyway, Eddie's wife packed up the kids and left him to it. She started again somewhere, but none of her old friends have kept in touch. For some reason, I had a notion he'd gone to Queensland, but now I find him here. Life's a funny old thing. I might have lost my daughter and her husband, but through that, I reconnect with you and Eddie. So, when one door closes...'

'...another one opens.' I didn't mean to finish her sentence, but it dawned on me, with all these killings, if someone was closing doors? Who was the beneficiary of whatever doors were being opened? I needed to see Eddie.

'Room okay?' I asked.

'Fine, but I don't want to put you out for long.'

'No trouble, to me. Besides there's a killer out there I need to catch.'

'About that,' she sounded sheepish, 'I played dumb to your friends. I didn't tell them much at all about Estelle's business. You, however, have a right to know.' She smiled at me, 'Come on, let's avenge my less than perfect daughter.'

CHAPTER FIFTEEN

Eddie was at the sink rinsing cups and stacking the dishwasher as I held the door for Donna. I'd decided to confront the elephant in the room before it grew any larger. 'Got a minute mate?' I asked.

'Donna, tell you who I was?' He was on to me straight away.

'She told me who you are. Should I be worried about the fact that you never bothered to tell me you knew Estelle's people?'

'Well, I knew Donna and George, but as for Luke and Estelle, only to wave at. My ex probably moved in their circle, but you'd have found me hanging out with the university kids most of the time. They were more fun and had no-one to impress. I didn't lie to you, Voss. I've been using the name of Eddie ever since I went bust.' He dropped his eyes and muttered. 'Never wanted to be Roger again.'

Eddie wasn't one to show emotion, but when he looked up I could see some welling in his eyes and felt his discomfort too. Sensing his self-esteem came from staying on the high side of the narrow line that separates failure from success, I decided to get back to the case.

'Glad we cleaned that up then. I wanted...'

He held his hand up, 'before you start, there's something more you should know.'

'What?' I was relieved he was back in control.

'Give me a chance and I'll tell you,' he looked at Donna and winked, 'you said you wanted someone to check over Luke's books and there'll be other paperwork to check too, right?'

'Yeah?' I didn't know where he was going with this.

'Well sitting in front of you is one of the best forensic accounting minds in the country.'

Donna's grin lit the room. 'Ta-da' she said and feigned a curtsey. 'Moi'

'So, if you trust Donna and, I think you can, we can expand our little crime fighting team and get this done. What say you?'

'Jesus Eddie, you're a manipulative prick.'

'He's right though,' Donna was beaming now, 'besides it would be nice to feel useful again. Estelle might have sent me money, but I never felt it was earned. If I help find her killer, well I won't feel as bad about it.'

'Yeah, okay, but it's just between the three of us, if Una gets just a whiff of what we're doing, my job's toast.'

'So, am I in?' She opened her hands and hung on the *in* until I said yes.

Eddie had conjured up a magnetic whiteboard from somewhere and set it up against the curtains that blacked out the room. The photocopier was still doing its thing, only this time there was no paper going through it.

'Do you mind if I bring in a stool from the kitchen?' Donna asked, 'I'm not as tall as you two and I'd like to try to get as close to level with your eye line as I can,'

'Go for it.' I said.

I stared at the photos and the way they'd been positioned. I knew there had to be logic in the sequence, but I couldn't see the pattern. I would have had different coloured lines linking them by now.

A warning chimed on the photocopier.

'Damn, I meant to override the paper jam warning when it's scanning, I'll be a tick, okay.'

'Yeah, sure,' I kept staring at the board.

'You need to know some things about Estelle that you won't find pleasant, Voss. Are you ready for it? I know how much she meant to you.'

Donna clattered the stool down to where she could see the board.

'Let's just find out who killed her first, eh?' I wanted to comfort her, not drag her daughter's name through the mud.

'It might be what got her killed Sam,' she shrugged, 'as I told you, Estelle was no innocent.'

'Everything's set to go,' Eddie slapped a hand on my shoulder, 'I could have put this onto a slide if I had a projector but couldn't find one for the right price.

'What is the right price?' Donna asked.

'He wanted someone to donate it,' I said.

'Oh, so that's how it works?'

'Anyway, the victims are all down the left, including your girl from last night.'

Donna clapped a hand over her mouth when she read the name. 'Patrice no? You silly young girl.'

I saw tears in her eyes and put my arm around her. 'Sorry, you knew her?'

'She worked for Estelle's modelling agency, a kind of talent scout. She went around the schools giving talks on career day, handing cards out, that type of thing. God Estelle, what have you done?' She dabbed her eyes with a tissue she took from the sleeve of her cardigan. 'Sorry Eddie, do go on.'

'Like I said, the victims are down the left. I've had the scanner working for the last day and in the columns going across the page are their connections in order of priority. If we have a photo, and we do for most, then they have their picture at the top. Now that you've brought Donna to our little party, I needed to add her in too.'

'What are the pictures below the line in the victim's column?' Donna asked.

I'd guessed, but Eddie answered for me. 'Potential victims.'

'That's me,' Donna slid off her stool and tapped the photo, 'going by this, you're saying I could be next.'

'That's why I brought you here,' I said, 'and Eddie's calculations just proved me right.'

'So why would anyone want to kill you, Donna?' Eddie asked the question I was reluctant to voice.

'Because I know too much, I suppose, but what is it that I'm supposed to know?'

My phone vibrated in my pocket. I took it out and listened. It was the Polynesian. 'Mr Raftopolous will see you at ten minutes past two. He'll send a car.'

'I'm at home.'

'We know.'

'I have company.'

'We know that too.'

'Two ten it is then.' I affirmed and put the phone away.

'Raftopolous?' Eddie asked as he plucked a sheet from the collator. 'Big time Sydney crime boss, father of the man we call Snake and associate of both Luke and Peter Peters.'

'Luke Peters?' I asked.

'Loan shark arrangement. If the client can't pay for, or should I say couldn't pay for Luke Peter's expenses, the old man made a loan available. Makes a lot of money out of it, does your Mr Raftopolous.' He passed me the sheet.

'Slimy bastard,' I said.

'Luke did pro-bono work, too,' Donna had anxiety in her voice.

'Not a lot,' I said, and passed her the paper.

'Let me get my bag,' she slid off her stool, 'I can give you the account numbers and access codes to all Estelle's banking.'

'And Luke's?' Eddie said.

'Only two,' Donna replied, 'he was a dope when it came to money. Everything they had came from Estelle.'

My ride turned up on time. Getting in a car with mobsters is not something I made a practice of, but Eddie had offered me a little protection. I chewed enough gum to choke a baboon. Inside the candy ball Eddie had hidden a tracking chip. I moved it around in my mouth for a few minutes and every time I spoke I made sure the words were garbled.

'Sorry,' I said and spat the gum into a tissue. I went to put it in the ashtray when Raftopolous pointed to a car tidy sitting behind the console, 'I had garlic and onions with lunch,' I added, by way of an excuse.

The old man grunted and then he slapped my leg. 'Wogs, like us don't smell it son,' his laugh rippled from his more than ample belly, creating a wave motion in his suit, 'we're going back to Sydney tonight and before we do, my son has something to tell you.'

'Okay, I'm ready to hear it,' I said.

'Son?' Raftopolous sounded keen to be finished with me.

'Mr Voss, I don't know anything, whoever is doing this is mad. I just pick up and deliver the movies to the addresses I'm given. Some of them are hotels or gyms or sports clubs. Others are for business people, politicians and embassy staff. Other than that, and checking the porn palace with Peter Peters, I can't tell you anything else.'

'And the car you were driving when I met you at the porn palace, as you called it?'

'Well that's what it is, you saw the shit in there. I tell you, those people think the girls on the street are trash.' I thought he was going to say more, but his father tapped the floor with his walking stick.

'Okay, but what about the car and the ammo and the bags of cocaine?'

'Not mine, it was rental I drove for Mr Peters,' his Adam's apple rose and fell as if he was trying to swallow a mouse, 'one of his fleet, I think.'

'You have it every day?'

'He collects me in it when the alarm goes off.'

'I think we're done now. Time to take you home.' Raftopolous tapped the Polynesian on the shoulder, the tyres squealed and we powered back the way we'd come.

'The bullets?'

'Not his,' Raftopolous sounded as if he'd lost patience with me, 'and take your rubbish with you,' he smiled, but it didn't quite reach his eyes, 'and say hello to Roger for me, eh.'

The car stopped outside the house. 'I'll stay in touch.' I said.

'No,' the old man said, 'it won't be necessary.'

The Polynesian held the door open and I was back into the sunlight.

CHAPTER SIXTEEN

There was so sign of Donna or Eddie inside the house. I went through to the courtyard to find the Cooper S missing, the shed locked, and the side gate secured. The buggers were driving around in my pride and joy and I was ready to kill them.

My phone vibrated again and a text message asked if I was home and ready to take delivery of my car. The damage must have been minor, but the way Una had described it the whole front end had been torn up. I confirmed the time for delivery and went back into inside to contemplate my next move.

The tow truck had arrived and as I stood in the street watching my car being unloaded I saw my Cooper S powering toward us. Donna was behind the wheel, she threw it into a slide and drifted it toward the back of the tilt-tray. The next moment the car was straight and with smoke coming from the front wheels she powered down the driveway. It took me a while to register what had happened.

'Sign here mate.'

'I haven't looked for damage yet,' the image of Donna driving my collector's piece affected my ability to take in the situation.

'No damage mate. I just had to pick it up and bring it here.'

'Who signed the order?' I still didn't get it.

'A female copper, plain clothes, Lucy Nguyen I think, here,' he passed me the paper he had in his hand, 'see for yourself.'

I gave it a cursory glance and passed it back. I was ropable. Eddie and Donna had driven out in an unregistered and uninsured car on public roads, not even touching on the fact that technically they'd stolen it. I wasn't proud of the tantrum I threw, but I felt better after it. Only then was I ready to listen.

Donna waved my outburst aside as if it meant nothing. 'I drove those things in the Southern Cross Rally back in the day and besides, it let me have a bit of fun while we went home to pick up my computer and a few things from the safe. Stuff that will help us to solve this.' Somehow, I had become the villain of the piece and I could see where Estelle had got her manipulative powers from. She threw me the keys and touched Eddie's elbow, 'come on, let's do this.'

'Gotta go,' he followed like a puppy at her heels, 'the lady's on a mission.'

The Cooper S smelled hot and clicked and creaked as it fought with the engine to contract at the same speed. I locked my safely returned pursuit car in the garage and joined the pair of rogues in the house.

'What was so important it couldn't wait?'

'Estelle asked me to help her set up a few offshore accounts over eight years ago. Everything is on this laptop she gave me.' Donna was not a woman to say sorry unnecessarily.

'And you said something about the safe?'

Eddie sat back and smiled. He was enjoying watching me ball out someone other than him and probably enjoying the futility of it even more. 'Tell him Donna, I can see he's making you wilt.'

'It'd take more than him to get me pissed off, Eddie. I learned from the best, George had a hell of a temper, but it was no match for mine. So, if you please Sam, here are the contents of the safe,' she slapped a copy of Estelle's will down in front of me and the letter she had written giving the solicitor her funeral instructions. She grabbed my ears and looked into my eyes, 'Sam, if you're spoiling for a fight, just let me know. My daughter is dead. Other people, both good or bad, are dropping like flies and I'm about pissed off enough to murder someone myself. Now I suggest you forget about your precious little car and help Eddie and me find who's doing this.'

I'd lost another battle and thinking Eddie was loving this, turned my attention to him. 'So what have we then?'

Eddie pointed back to his power point screen. 'If you look closely you'll see who has the most connections from those on the board.'

'Luke, then Estelle,' Donna shrugged, 'they were always popular, but I'd never expected it to be this way.'

'Luke only makes the cut because he's represented the people in court. Take out the court cases and he drops to the bottom of the list. If the cases he won are deleted, he wouldn't have even been on the list. I reckon he was tortured to make her talk.'

'Not me,' I said, 'he was up to his neck in something and whatever it was got them both killed.'

'Sam,' Donna turned me to face her again,' Estelle was not the woman you married. She was an invasive, noxious weed of a person before she died. She might have been my daughter and I loved her, but over the last five or so years I saw how destructive she'd become.' She wasn't pulling any punches today. 'Put the memory stick in Eddie, he'll have to see it for himself.' On her way out of the room she turned and said. 'You won't mind excusing me. I've seen it once and I never want to see it again.'

I watched about five minutes of a porn movie before I, too, had had enough. 'Turn it off. I get it now.' Estelle had been the star of the production. A menu page showed a list of the other players and it seemed as if a good number of Canberra's elite also had a role. 'We can look at this as a blackmailer wanting to free themselves from being bled dry.'

'The list's a long one,' Donna said as she returned.

'Not to my...' Eddie stumbled for something to call his contraption.

'Let's refer to as VU-3 for now. That stands for Voss Undercover and the three of us,' Donna smiled, 'are you going to tell your boss what we've discovered?'

I winked at her suggestion. 'Tell her what? That you have a home movie? I don't know that she'd be interested so how about we do a bit more work first?'

'Thanks.' She said.

'Luke Peters got her into it.' I said this louder than I intended and Eddie raised his eyebrows.

'Not guilty,' Donna said, 'not this time.' She tapped my arm, 'you have to stop thinking about him as the bloke who stole your wife and start looking at her without those bloody rose-coloured glasses she blinded you with. My daughter or not, Estelle was a long way from perfect. Got it?'

I nodded.

'Good, now if you two concentrate on the possibility of blackmail and I'll trace the money.' She gathered up her batted old suit case full of papers and went to the dining room table. 'I'm in here until you need me.'

'Do you need my laptop?' My words trailed after her.

'Nope, I do things the old-fashioned way. You probably call it analogue these days, but when I started pencil and paper did the trick.'

Eddie was typing the names listed in the DVD credits into his database and I seemed to be as handy as a cigarette lighter on a Jet Ski. 'Reckon I'll drop by Gabby's office, and see if she can tell me anything about that arrow.'

He leant back in his chair and pulled a few papers from a pile on the printer, 'I hacked her report. Everything's here.'

'Shit Eddie, we could spend years inside for this.'

'If you don't tell, then they won't know.' He did his eyebrow dance again.

'You know the old Mafia saying about two people keeping a secret, don't you?' He shook his head. 'A secret's only safe, when one of the last two people keeping it, is dead.'

'Yeah, but we're not the Mafia.' He smiled, 'don't go anywhere unusual in the car, eh.'

'No, why?'

'Una's had it bugged. Drive around a bit, but don't use your phone or go anywhere you don't want her to know about.' He grinned again, 'I'll knock up a jammer and install a loop for it later.'

'The cheeky bitch,'

'Well you slipped that ball of gum with the bug in it somewhere on Raftopolous' limo.'

'Up under the rear wheel arch, and he's a crim and I'm not.'

He smiled at me in that screwed up face of his. 'Yeah, well I tried to find out if it was leased or stolen. Seems the old man paid cash for it in Sydney.'

I was a detective at the top of my game with a killer to catch, only every turn I took seemed to leave me blocked and now Donna had worked her way into my clandestine investigation. I was beginning to feel like a dog on a chain. If I was shut out of the official investigation and had nothing much to offer with what Eddie and Donna were doing, maybe I could take coffee to my old team as a bit of a peace offering.

I decided to call in on Peter Peters on my way, for no other reason than if Una had bugged the car, then I wanted to see how she'd react if I tried to put Peters under the blow torch for a while.

He must have given whoever usually stood guard at his office door the afternoon off, because it was open. I sauntered in and took a seat at his desk. He had his back to the desk, staring out over the roof tops and I sat there for at least two minutes before he turned away from the window.

'Shit!' He took two steps back tripping over his chair and falling onto his arse. I didn't get up. 'What the fuck do you want?'

'I want to know everything you and Estelle were into. I know about the porn and the blackmail and if I look deep enough, I reckon I can find a couple of pushers who will swear an oath that you not only supplied them but got them into it in the first place.'

'Bullshit, you can't do that.'

'I'm off the case and desperate and I can call on a dozen people who'll give me an alibi if I have to throw you under a bus. So yeah, I'm confident Superintendent Knight would believe anything I told her.' I picked up a pencil from his desk tray and rolled it between my fingers. 'So, what have you got for me?'

'Nothing. Christ Voss, I have no idea where Estelle made her money. I pleaded for Luke to invest in the factory precinct. He turned me down, said it would compromise his position.'

'But you got the cash from him in the end?'

'I was pissed off with him, threw my whisky glass into his fireplace and stormed out. I mean, what kind of a brother turns you down at every opportunity? He was mean as a kid, took anything he wanted and had no respect for anyone,' he grinned at me, 'but I don't have to tell you that, now, do I?'

He watched me. I gave him nothing.

He sat in his chair and leant his elbows on the desk. 'A few days later and I get a call from Estelle, said she had some money to invest and could I meet her and her business adviser.'

'And who was that?'

'Didn't give a name and I didn't ask. All I know is that the money came into my account from a bank in the Cayman Islands. My only problem was that along with the money came a partner, and Estelle was definitely not a silent partner.'

'And you didn't want her involved.'

'Shit no, she was a complete pain in the arse. That whole warehouse, slash, film set was the only reason she found the money.'

'And the limousines?'

'Yeah, that's something that worked out though. The security company was all hers, but we had a deal about that bloody film set. If an alarm went off, I had to gather up Raftopolous Junior and check it out. The number of times we went in and it was nothing. All of the fucking time. When I got done for drink driving I gave Junior the car and left it to him to gather me up. I don't know what it was he was up to. As I told your slope and her sidekick, I knew nothing about the coke or the gun.'

I cringed at the word, slope, and slapped him across the side of the head. 'If I ever hear you say anything about my colleague like that again, or anyone else for that matter, it won't be just the one hit. Got it?'

'Christ Voss, Yes,

'There was a gun?' I thought back to the ammo and the white powder, but I hadn't seen a gun.

'Apparently?'

'There, that wasn't so hard, was it?' I watched him rub the welts that were rising from my hand print.

'Piss off.'

'So Lucy, she knows about the business?'

'Probably more than me. One thing I can tell you for free is that Estelle knew who was who. Where the money was and what she needed to do to get it.'

'Is that what got her killed?'

'All of the above, shit Voss, how the hell would I know?'

I saw sweat beading across his forehead and the way he mopped it with a white handkerchief reminded me of a Danny DeVito mannerism in the movie Other People's Money. In fact, in certain profile, he could have passed as the actor's double.

'The only thing that scares me more than the killer, is prison, so I'm helping okay? You know, you just being here makes me nervous. More than once you've called on someone and next minute they're dead too.' He squirmed in his chair and made sure I could see his eyes. 'If you find the bastard before the cops do, don't be a hero. Take them out, don't buggerise around, just do it.'

I stood up and wondered if I'd frightened him enough and in case I hadn't, offered some advice. 'Stay away from the window. Whoever's doing the killing could hit a golf ball at three hundred meters.' I walked through the door and smiled to the sound of curtains being closed.

CHAPTER SEVENTEEN

I swung by a Fyshwick firearms dealer. I wanted to handle a crossbow to understand what was involved in loading it and how much time was needed to take out the target. I came away with a head full of information that only confused me, but I had a place and a contact who could show me how to use the weapon.

A phone call later and I had a test set up for two days' time, along with a list of club members and the weapons and arrows they used. I knew the crossbows were silent killers, a velocity of well over three hundred feet per second adding to the killing potential. The gun shop was going to email the information to me.

A Mud Bucket drive through coffee place was close to my office and often quiet at this time of day, so I swung in behind a grey Mercedes CLK 350 and crept forward at glacial pace. The women in the convertible were on something other than coffee. If I'd been on the job and not under suspension, I'd be tempted to do my bit for society and pull them over for a breath test. Without that option, I phoned a colleague in traffic and suggested they attend the Mud Bucket pronto.

Before the women got their coffee, a patrol car pulled in and two officers began breath testing the line. The Mercedes driver was more than a touch agitated, throwing her handbag at the officer when he asked for her licence. I smiled to myself. She'd pose no danger to other road users for the rest of the day. As the other women seemed in no state to drive either, one of the officers moved the car out of the drive thru lane. I was just ordering my coffee when the passenger door opened.

'Be a sport mate, run us back to our hotel yeah?' She was about thirty, tattered around the edges, and her breath reeked of cigarettes and booze.

I screwed my face up with the blast of it all.

She waved her hand as if she was moving smoke. 'Pffft, don't take a lot of notice of us. We're all a bit stonkered. One of our mates was murdered last night, can you believe it? Murdered! We thought we'd drown our sorrows and now it looks like Julie's headed for the pokey, oops. We should have thought it through I suppose.'

By now she was in the passenger seat, her friend was in the back and my head was reeling at the serendipitous turn of events. There'd only been one homicide in Canberra in the past twenty-four house and that had been Patrice.

'Anyway, it's real nice of you to take us. We sure can use a friend right now. Can't we, Leah?'

I hadn't recalled agreeing to take them as I paid for my order and progressed to the next window to collect the drinks, but this opportunity was too good to pass on.

'Well now that you've carjacked me, where is your hotel?'

'Rydges, you know the one?' Leah slurred the words at me. 'Handy you were here to rescue us, eh Steph?'

'Okay, Rydges it is. You said you lost a friend, how did it happen?'

'She was at some posh function and someone shot her with an arrow. What kind of sick bastard does that?' Steph sounded both angry and sad. She took a coffee out of the tray and passed it back to Leah, my plans to pay take a surprise coffee to Una and Lucy had gone. 'Thanks for this,' she said raising her cup in a toast, 'want yours now?'

'Not while I'm driving, thanks all the same.' I looked in the mirror at Leah, she was either gazing into space or looking at her reflection in the window, I couldn't tell which.

'She was only supposed to be there for a little while too,' Leah had been listening after all. 'We drew straws to see who would go last night. Christ, first it's Estelle and now Patrice. I wish the cops would find this bastard, none of us are safe while he's still out there.'

'Shh Leah, the gentleman doesn't need to hear our troubles,' Steph patted my knee, 'like a knight riding in on a white charger to rescue the fair maiden, aren't you?' She patted my knee again then started a laugh and blew coffee into her hand. I pulled a couple of tissues from the pack I kept in the console and handed them to her, 'although it's been a long time since any of us could say we were fair or maidens though, eh girl?'

Quite apart from their intoxicated state, their speech didn't match their manner of dress, an upmarket couture of a kind sold by Xirena Zelazny Designs. I wondered if the next part of their rambling conversation might tick that box.

'Estelle might have taught us to talk posh and walk like ladies, but she also showed us how to…'

'Not in front of …'

'Voss,' I said.

'Hey,' Steph said, 'you must have known Estelle. She was married to a Voss once and it's not a common name.'

Leah slipped out of her seat belt and I felt her face near my ear. 'Did you know Estelle?'

'I knew Estelle a long time ago, yes, and how about we put your seatbelt back on, yeah?'

'And you're a copper, if I remember?' Leah had lost most of the posh from her voice.

'Suspended.' I said.

'What did you do to get the push?' She was now twisted in her belt and facing me. 'Did you piss off some higher ups?'

'No, nothing like that, I'm a bit close to the investigation that's all,' I wondered if I could press them more, 'just what was Estelle teaching you?'

'Well we came to her modelling agency to try and be, you know, famous. Estelle had a reputation for getting her models into some of the best photo shoots. Say a model's name.' I could feel Leah warming to me.

'Sorry, I don't have much to do with that line of work.'

'Go on who's the most famous Aussie model you've read about?' Steph said, 'say a name and I'll bet Estelle helped her on her way.'

'You know that TV show, Footballers Wives,' Leah said, 'or that one about outback blokes looking for love. The producers of those shows always looked to Estelle for talent. If they do any good, she gets a finder's fee and a percentage of their earnings as their manager. Patrice was her number two, sort of like a deputy, and now she's gone too, I don't know what'll happen to all of us now.'

The hotel doorman opened Leah and Steph's doors at the same time. Leah's designer dress had worked its way upwards to bunch around her waist as she slid out and she took her time in smoothing it down. 'Wanna come up for a while? We'll be here until the day after next. Room three-o-five.'

'Thanks all the same, but I'd better get back to my afternoon.'

'Well, thanks for the ride anyway, here's my mobile number if I can do anything to repay you,' Leah leaned in the window and pressed a card into my hand, 'anything at all.'

I watched them go inside, parked the car and slipped a twenty to the doorman as I asked, 'the girls I just dropped off. What can you tell me?'

'Hi class Toms. Pity how good looking kids like them get into the trade.' He shook his head. 'I've got daughters too, thankfully none of them have fallen into the trap of entertaining visiting dignitaries.' He looked me up and down. 'Sorry you are?'

'No, I'm not a client, I work with the police,' I felt in my pocket for a badge or something to show him before remembering my suspension, 'their friend was driving drunk and the cops took her off the road,' I smiled, 'I guess they needed to get back here somehow and I was convenient, that's all. Do you happen to know who their pimp is?'

'Nope, a limo dropped them off a week ago. It comes and goes, usually the girls work in pairs.'

'Always in pairs?'

'Sometimes they would all go off together.'

'Never alone.'

He looked at the sky as if searching for an answer. 'No, never on their own. Not that I've seen anyway. Sometimes they've left with another woman.'

'How often do they use this hotel?'

'Four or five times a year, I suppose. The desk would have it on record,' he clapped me on the shoulder, 'and they always ask for the same suite.'

'Thanks,' I said, 'you've been a big help.' It was time to see Una, but not before I found out how Julie was getting home.

My newly processed drunk driver was waiting for a ride back to the hotel. I spoke to the desk and said I'd be prepared to drive her. I explained how I knew her friends and she called them to verify my word. Julie wasn't concerned about her car. It belonged to a hire company and they were arranging to have it collected.

'Did the girls tell you what we do?' Her words were slurred, but nowhere as bad as her companions, 'God, once they get a bit of bubbly in them they run off at the mouth.'

I walked her to my car and opened the rear door.

'If it's all the same with you, I'll ride up front. In our line of work most people want us either in the back where they can't see us, or on their arm to show everyone they can pull a pretty face.'

When she said the name of the hire company, Estelle's name was forefront again. 'How did you get involved with Estelle?'

'I'm a dreamer. A lot of people think Sydney and Melbourne are the centre of the fashion world, but Canberra has an intense model presence. Estelle was the best talent spotter in Australia,' she crossed and uncrossed her legs, 'some of us make it, most of us didn't.'

'And those who don't make it?'

'Some go on and marry pretty men, most of us do escort work for a while,' she let out a sigh, 'it becomes a habit and we end up here, not that it's too bad most of the time, but some of the johns,' she shook her head as if shaking dirt from her hair, 'they could leave you in hospital. They're the hard days.'

'Why not just chuck it all in and do an office job or something?'

'All of us want the dream, you know. If I couldn't be a model, maybe I could meet some of the eligible diplomat bachelors, travel the world, settle down and raise a couple of beautiful kids,' she paused, 'Christ, I wish I'd stayed in Cooma.'

I helped her out of the car at the hotel, asked the doorman to watch it for me and walked her to the lift. 'Three-oh-five, isn't it?'

'Yeah, you want to walk me up?'

'If you want, sure, it'll be nice.'

I knocked on the door and Leah opened it, now dressed in track pants and a tee. I left them and headed down the elevator and off to see Una, the name of the Escort service in my pocket.

CHAPTER EIGHTEEN

Una did not look pleased, 'Voss, what the hell are you doing? You shouldn't be here.' She looked flustered, the veneer of control slipping, 'I can't have you in here. This case is all over the place, we don't know if the killer has a plan, or if there is more than one murderer out there and you being here only muddies the water. This isn't your local drop in for a chat joint, we're in the middle of a murder case and you're under suspension in case you've forgotten.'

'You need help.'

'You're not telling me anything I don't know, but as usual we're short of feet on the ground.' She glared at me as if I was somehow responsible for all the shortcomings of the department.

'So, it would be better if I shot through and left you to it?'

'Yes, just go Voss. I don't need you hovering around acting like some sort of superior knowledge font.'

'Know much about the girl, Patrice, yet?'

'I can't tell you that.'

'No, but just maybe I could tell you a thing or two, but not here. Maybe you can buy me dinner for scratching my car and we can talk then.'

'Time would be a nice thing?'

'I'll pick you up about seven and I'll even buy if that moves you.'

'Make it eight. I've got to wrangle with the Assistant Commissioner later. He's not at all pleased that a woman

129

died at a function I attended,' she wiped the back of her hand across her brow, 'and having you dive in to try and rescue her hasn't helped either.'

'You probably owe me a new suit as well. The list of IOUs gets bigger every day.'

'I don't like your chances. Now get out of here.'

Trying to hide my elation at her inability to replace me, I left her office. From what I could work out, they were swamped with clues, but they had nothing to tie a suspect to. Feeling superior was not something I usually allowed myself, but tonight I felt I had more of an idea about this case than those working on it legitimately. I had Eddie who, rightly or wrongly, was able to access almost anyone's database and in Donna, I had a forensic accountant working on my shadow team. All I needed was a forensic pathologist and I had the makings of a private investigation office.

By the time I pulled into my drive, I realised I was singing to the radio. Smooth FM might play golden oldies, but even I could suspend time with most of the tunes. My mood buoyed, I was ready to learn what my two super-sleuths had unearthed. I didn't realise it, but I was whistling when I reached the control hub.

'Someone's happy,' Donna too, sounded as if she'd won the lottery, 'come and have a look at this.'

'Estelle told me she had some money salted away for a rainy day, but it seems with all of the stuff she had on the go, the little bugger had planted a field full of money trees.'

'Is any of it legal?' To me, anyone who made money paid tax, a lot of tax. I took the A4 sheet she passed me. I was staring at numbers and names in a hierarchal chart, not understanding any of it.

'Every bit of it.' Eddie said. 'She may have worked the system to her own advantage, but even the money transfers and offshore companies are up to date with their tax obligation. As Donna said, she may not have been an angel, but her paperwork was precise.'

'Okay, none of this tells me why she was killed though.' I looked at lines of code on one of the screens, an endless scrolling of names numbers and addresses.

Eddie pointed to the screen. 'See the scrolls are starting to slow, when they stop, you'll see a probability ratio of better than one in a hundred.'

'Christ that's only one percent. I can guess better than that.'

Donna patted my shoulder. 'He's being modest. What Eddie means is, from Australia's phone book, he'll have one hundred names.' She smiled at him. 'That's much better than one percent.'

The other screen was scrolling registration numbers, car models, addresses, dates and times. I thought whatever he was trying was a longshot, but so far we had little hard evidence and anything his experiment pulled up would not work in a court room. However, I realised it could point me in the right direction.

'Donna, I want you to show me everything you have on the modelling agency,' I kept staring at the names on the organisational chart, 'that girl who died last night was one of her team.'

'I'd hoped we wouldn't need to look into that, it's a bit...'

'Unsavoury.' Eddie finished her sentence. 'Do we have to?'

'Yeah, if you want to take a minute to yourself while we follow the trail, I'll understand, but it is important. We can't do anything to help Estelle, but we might be able to stop her killer from harming anyone else.' I put an arm around her, she melted into me and quietly sobbed against my shoulder. I'd forgotten the fragility she'd often hid behind a tough exterior.

Eddie motioned to us and I stood behind Donna's chair to look at the activity on the far screen. 'All the limos are rolling.'

'They work every day, should be nothing special about that?'

'Yeah but they're converging on the film set.' I watched him type something. He may have only used a few fingers, but his hands were a blur when he used the keyboard. 'Something on you reckon?'

'Will they all arrive at the same time?'

'Hang on,' he typed ETA and pointed to dots that signalled the different cars, 'there should only be one car arriving and leaving at a time. Why would you do that?'

'They don't want the occupants to see each other.' Donna had composed herself and re-joined the conversation. 'Do we know where each limo picked up and what time?'

'It'll take me a minute or two, but yeah, I can work that out,' he was already typing as he spoke.

'Donna, if Estelle's business interests were as wide and varied as you say they are then she must have had someone other than the solicitor and accountant managing everything. Do you know who or can you find out where I should start looking?' I asked.

'Tobias Rosen. He works from their office in Sydney. I'll find you all the details.'

'Good stuff. Just how rich was your daughter?' Eddie asked Donna.

Donna shrugged and looked at the ceiling. 'I don't know, at one time Luke complained he was married to a woman who was richer than God. I didn't know what he meant. It was a few years after they started living in separate rooms,' she sighed, 'not a happy union, and

Estelle only stayed to maintain her position in society. Her work took her all over the world at times. I thought it was just the fashion side, but when you look at this,' she waved the hierarchal chart at me, 'I didn't know my daughter at all.'

'More money than God, eh?' I loved that phrase.

'It's what he said. I didn't think much of it back then, and I find it hard to believe now.' She spun back to her screen and started searching for organisational charts and end of year reports for each of Estelle's companies.

'Here,' Eddie passed me a list, 'sure you want to see this?'

The limos had picked up from some of the best Canberra addresses and some of the names lined up with those from the DVD credits. I knew the press would have a field day if they knew what was happening and even supposition could ruin the careers of several high-profile Australians.

I looked at my watch. Time to pick up Una.

CHAPTER NINETEEN

Una was tapping her watch, when I arrived.

I checked the station clock. 'Two minutes,' I said.

'It wouldn't hurt you to be punctual. Now take me somewhere no one will see us and get me a long cold drink.' Manners had never been her strong point.

I walked her to the car and opened the door. She sat down and fixed her eyes on the windscreen. For as much as I was taking her out, she seemed not in the mood for pleasantries. I drove over to Braddon. I'd read about a French restaurant, Les Bistronomes, in the good food guide. The article said it had a great reputation and besides, I liked French food.

The carpark was almost empty and the bistro quiet, which should have pleased my dinner companion. I turned the car off and walked to the passenger door and opened it. She sat there, unmoving.

'Ready?' I held out my hand for her to take.

'Mind if we don't?' She asked, 'I'd really prefer a Vegemite sandwich and a cup of tea.'

'You are joking, aren't you?' She could have said something on the drive over, or when I had picked her up would have been even better.

'Nope, take me home, I don't think I can do this tonight.' This was Una at her finest, the absolute queen of control.

The ride home was frosty. I had no idea of the reason behind her change of mood. Trying to gauge an understanding of what was going on, I asked a couple of questions unrelated to the case. She said nothing, just turned away from me and looked out of the window. At home, she sat in the car and waited for me to open the door for her. This was a habit that had to stop and I made a mental note to remind myself the next time. At the front door, she passed me her key and waited while I opened it, my recent resolve forgotten so quickly. I followed her in, 'Turn the lights on and make yourself comfortable, I'm going to change.'

I went through into the kitchen and looked in the fridge. Una might have been happy with a vegemite sandwich but it wouldn't make up for the French cuisine my taste buds had been primed for. Eddie thought I was hopeless, well he should have looked in here. There was enough to make an omelette, but not much more. I checked the best before date on the carton and decided it might be best to crack each egg into a cup first. The freezer hid a few frozen vegies and diced ham. It wouldn't be the best meal in the world, but a few leaves salvaged from a browning lettuce and a couple tomatoes proved a bonanza.

Una came back into the room running a towel through her hair as I set two places at the table. In flannel pyjamas and with wet hair, she was attractive in a sisterly sort of way.

'Sorry about tonight. I've just had a shitty couple of hours. God Voss, how do you put up with the continual scrutiny?'

'I have you shielding me from above, the rest of it I let go. Only people I care about can hurt me.'

'Can I hurt you?' She propped an elbow on the table and rested her chin on it.

'Often.'

'And?'

'And I forgive you and move on. It's too hard for me to carry a grudge and work too.'

'How many people on your list of those who hurt you?'

'Not many. I have a reputation to keep.'

'Estelle was one, though?'

'Omelette?' I wanted to get away from this conversation. 'It's the best I can do with what's you had the fridge.'

'Better than stale toast and a cup of soup.' She smiled at me, while I beat the eggs. 'It's nice to have someone who cares.'

'Want to talk about it?'

'Oh, what the hell. You're not going to say anything.' She slid up onto a stool on the other side of the bench. 'The Assistant Commissioner has put me on notice. If I don't get a result soon, or at least find a line of enquiry that leads to an arrest, I'm to be relieved. Lucy is up to her ears with this. She's under tremendous pressure and, no matter how good she is, she's not you.'

I allowed myself a smile, the meal was almost ready. 'Do you want me to pull your chair out ma'am?'

'Oh, piss off Voss. I can sit on a chair without your help.'

'Just checking?' I loaded omelette onto our plates and carried them to the table.

'I know you won't tell me about the case, so do you want to tell me why you're sulking like a spoilt kid?'

I knew my timing was off the minute the words left my mouth. She dropped her fork, it clattered onto the plate and food scattered over the placemat. She narrowed her eyes. 'Forget it, you're like every other man I know, I thought you were someone who didn't judge. Show yourself out, I'm going to bed.'

'Hey hang on, I'm friend, not foe.' I waved my hand as a white flag of truce. Bugger it, I was asking for a ceasefire. The strongest woman I knew now looked like a castle whose walls had been breached. 'I'm sorry, but you have to admit, you aren't the same focussed woman I saw a few hours ago. Just tell me what's on your mind,' I pouted my lips and mimicked an old tutor of ours, 'c'mon tell old Uncle Sam what's wrong?'

'Piss off Voss,' She leaned an elbow on the table, turned to me and put her chin in her hand again. 'I've got another murder on my hands. I can't tell if it's related other than the victim was known to your ex.'

'And Luke Peters?' I wasn't ready to let him off the hook just yet.

'Possibly, but we know from the witness statements they knew each other. The latest victim, Patrice no-last-name-as-yet, worked either with, or for a company Estelle had an interest in.'

I wanted to drop Luke Peters name again but decided against it. I wanted to know how much the team knew. 'What was it Patrice did, exactly?'

'Some kind of concierge, we don't have a definitive job description.'

I wanted to throw her a bit of information, but just what to say yet, I wasn't sure. 'Want me to theorise?'

'What, no. I can't have you anywhere near this,' she picked up her fork and cut a corner off her omelette then curiosity must have got the better of her. 'Why, what ideas do you have?'

'I'd go down the blackmail track. I reckon one of the Peters and yes, I mean Luke, Peter, or Estelle, was putting a squeeze on someone who uses, or used that film set. You have keys that were secreted away. It's a sleazy industry and my guess is something happened that someone wants covered up.'

'Shit you're predictable. Lucy told me that's what you suspected from day one.' Her toughness was returning. 'We still have bodies turning up though. Why is that happening?'

'They haven't found what they are looking for yet.'

'And Peter Peters, why isn't he dead?'

'He might be the killer?'

She laughed and pointed her fork at me, 'he tried to point the finger at you, remember.'

'Covering his arse?'

'Nope, he's scared too. He even had a word with the secretary to the Minister, that's why I got my fingers rapped today. You're right though, he is a grubby little man, but he's no killer. What was it you said, soft?'

'So what links all the victims together? You must have something?'

'Only the hire cars,' she picked up her glass and sipped, 'however, it's also the most random clue.'

'Or the most important,' I raised my glass as if making a toast, 'good to have you back Ma'am.

'Don't shit me Voss, I never left.

'You reckon?' I leaned over to pat her shoulder.

She grabbed my hand. 'Touch me again and I'll break your fingers.'

I pulled back and smiled.

'One word of this and...'

'Look everyone needs a bit of...' She put her finger on my lips. I said no more and we finished our dinner in silence.

With the bottle of wine drained, she cleared the table and loaded the dishwasher. Una sounded relaxed and chatty as we had a caffeine nightcap. I had intended to share more information with her and suggested as much when I'd asked her to dinner, but she seemed to have forgotten. In hindsight, our covert operation and Eddie's ability to make the computer search and find almost anything was more than I wanted to explain at this point.

'Why did you pick up Estelle's mum after the last murder?'

'I didn't want to have her death on my conscience, I suppose,' I smiled at the image I had of the way she slid my Mini Cooper into the driveway, 'she's pretty feisty, though. I'm not sure I'd tackle her.'

'Is she handy in the kitchen?'

'I don't even go in there anymore. I should never have invited Eddie in either, he's become a tyrant and between the two of them I don't have a chance.' I laughed as if to show I was joking and wished I was.

'You're too soft to leave him out there for another winter. Anyway, I think it's nice, you've lived alone for way too long.'

'What about you?'

'Women are better on their own anyway, I've married enough losers to last me more than one life time.' She smiled and played with her hair. 'I never could get you to find me attractive enough though, could I?'

'Oh I find you attractive enough, believe me.'

'But?'

I laughed at her. 'You're like a sister to me and you know it. A bossy sister at that.'

She laughed as I walked to the door and turned to say goodbye, her hand reached up and she pulled my head down to kiss my cheek. 'Thanks brother,' she said, as I walked to the car. In the rear-view mirror, I watched the light from the front door disappear. I guessed she'd closed it.

At home, VU-3 was still scrolling, Donna was on the phone and Eddie had his head buried inside the pages of a hunting and fishing magazine I'd picked up at the gun shop. Everything was as expected.

Donna put the phone down. 'Early start tomorrow, I've told Tobias to clear his diary. A private plane will fly us to Sydney and he's arranged a car to meet us,' she passed me a piece of paper, 'I want to know everything the little minx had going. I'll call you at six.' She put her hand under my chin. 'Close your mouth Sam, it doesn't become you.'

Eddie was grinning at me, his eyebrows doing their little wiggle dance. 'Good luck, you'll find out everything from this Tobias bloke tomorrow, but I don't think it was blackmail that got her killed.'

'No?'

'We've exhausted that line of enquiry and there are no corresponding cash transfers. I can look deeper, but getting past these consulates and banking firewalls will bring some unwanted attention our way. So far, all attacks have been routed through several unsecured offshore internet cafes. I hope no one figures it out before I can bury it in the dark web.'

'What made Donna make the call?'

'She found something in Estelle's accounts. Got all fired up,' he made a movement like a dog shaking, 'and she frightened old Toby into sending the company jet for you.'

I wanted to ask Donna more, but as the shower was running I decided to wait until morning.

How had Estelle put away enough money to own a company jet?

I shook my head. It wasn't possible, Eddie had to have heard wrong.

CHAPTER TWENTY

Donna was reading the paper and half way through her toast when I made it to the kitchen, Eddie's snoring let the district know he was still in his room. I decided on toast too. I didn't want to risk dribbling cornflakes down my shirt.

'See this?' Donna turned the paper my way. The headline declared the investigating team were hopeless. 'You'd better do something to help your friends before everyone's out of work?'

'All down to me, is it?'

She smiled and patted my hand. 'George always said you might be frosty and aloof, but if anyone could bring a killer to justice, it'd be you.'

'He could have been gilding the lily a bit, you know how George McGuigan could paint a pretty picture of even the blackest heart.' I tried to take off her late husband's accent, but it was a poor imitation.

Donna picked up the thread and responded with kind. 'Poor Una, you're the only one who can save her. If the press doesn't have her head, the higher ups will.'

'And what power will you grant me, oh wise one?'

'Forget all this computer rubbish Eddie has bamboozled you with.' She was back to the old Donna. 'Use your head man, think about it, and put yourself in the killer's shoes. I think that's what you told George and me once. You said you tried to re-enact the killings as if you were inside the killer's head. If you saw,' she made speech marks with her fingers, 'how the murders had been done, it helped you understand why.'

'I said that?'

'Something like it, mind you it was after a big case and you were young and wanting to impress us.' She put her dishes on the sink. 'Be a love and fix mine when you do yours, eh?'

The airport was bustling with commuters. At the door to departures we were met by a young man in uniform carrying a sign with Donna's name on it. He ushered us to an airport vehicle that took us to a waiting Cessna Citation. Apart from the name, Estelle, scrolled into a gold leaf pin stripe along the plane's flanks, this was just another rich kid's toy.

The steps were down and we were ushered into the cabin to find three men already in the jet.

'Mrs Mcguigan, Mr Voss, I'm Tobias Rosen.' His two lieutenants flanked him but he by-passed introductions. 'Some of what we need to discuss is highly sensitive and it's probably better to talk freely away from the office. Leon and Frank here have put together a presentation of just what Estelle International is and what we are about. I thought we could watch it now and answer any questions you might have while on our way to lunch. I have a table booked for a luncheon near one of our investments in Adelaide.'

Donna gave me a look that let me know she was less than impressed with Mr Rosen. 'And all this is for our benefit?' She asked.

'Now that poor Estelle is no longer with us, I'm afraid you are eighty percent of our share-holding.'

'Okay,' she said, 'let's get this bird airborne and you can show me your presentation. Then after lunch, we can talk about finance and how you or we, as it now happens to be, fund this extravagance.'

'You have my complete co-operation.' Rosen's answers were spit polished and it was easy to see how he greased his way to the top of the corporate pile. 'We have nothing to hide.'

'Before we get started with the presentation, we'd like a list of all the girls who came to Estelle with a dream of being models. Every name from day one until today,' I said.

'Sure, why?' Rosen asked the question while his cohorts remained silent.

'I'm looking for a killer and she might be in that list.'

'You only want the girls?

'Are there men on the list?'

'Sure, we never made as much money as we did with the girls, but that's just peculiar to the industry.'

I scrawled an email address on a notepad and passed it across. 'Send the data to this address, names, addresses, age, history etcetera. Photos if you have them.'

'It may take a while,' Leon said, 'I'll send the names first and the complete resumes after, if that's okay with you?'

'Just do it.' Rosen said.

'What can you tell me about Patrice and the girls staying at Rydges?'

'I'm not sure I can help with that,' Rosen looked at Leon.

'I'll find out, while Frank gets on with the presentation.' He turned and went into an alcove at the rear of the plane.

I didn't bother to tell him Patrice was dead. I wanted to witness his reaction when he found out and watch his face when he explained her death to his boss.

For the next two hours we sat through a corporate lovefest. This presentation was a one size fits all job and I could see Donna was unimpressed.

'Thanks for the glossy magazine,' she said, 'but it doesn't tell me anything, Tobias. I like the grubby stuff, not the dream of where you want the company to be. I want the figures, the loss areas, the dogs. All the smutty-shitty stuff you want to hide from us,' she smiled, 'you see, all my life I've looked for the crap. It excites me.'

'Your daughter bragged about her badass mother.'

Donna smiled, 'badass, I like it.'

'Where did Luke Peters fit into all of this?' I knew he had to have put the money up to start this extravagance.

'Estelle made sure he had nothing to do with this. We were not to talk to him or show him anything. This is all Estelle. She started with little and worked hard. I came along and we built an international investment company,' he shook his head, 'I don't know what he did to piss her off, but she excluded him from everything.'

'Dipped his pen in too many inkwells, including a lot of her friends.' Donna said. This was the first-time Donna had said anything disparaging about Luke Peters. I wanted to press her for more, but didn't need too as she continued, 'it coincided with her first attempt at making movies, I checked the date on the DVD myself.'

'How did she fund her start?' I directed the question to Tobias.

'I'm not sure. I only came along when she needed help pulling all the ends of her empire together. When we formed Estelle International, she used her influence to find members who made up a strong board. The company already had an office in the Caymans as part of her modelling agency. She asked me to oversee the commercial structure to ensure we were maximising our opportunities and minimising our taxation liability.'

'Dodging tax in other words?' Donna suggested, one eyebrow raised in question.

'No, everything we do is completely legal. I can assure you we have nothing to fear from any tax department anywhere in the world,' he smiled like a car salesman greeting a client.

'So, is the business still built on smut?' Donna asked bluntly, as if she needed to confront the dirt, 'or is there some good in all of this?'

I sat back and watched the show, unsure if she was playing Tobias along, or genuinely wanted to know if pornography was the mainstay of the company.

'The presentation showed you our finance streams, if I can just ask Frank to bring them up again...'

'If you want our cooperation in the future then stop treating me like a little old lady.' She cut him short. 'I managed to keep a philandering husband in line so a pussy like you doesn't stand a chance,' the look she gave him was withering, 'I'll give you a couple of minutes to think about it and then after a chat with Frank and Leon, you can start again. Just stop bullshitting us and we'll all get along fine,' she looked about the plane,' and can someone get me a coffee please.'

I heard the engines winding down and looked out the window. We were North East of the Adelaide and banking. Rosen would have a little more time before he needed to explain. Donna leaned over and winked at me, crooking her little finger out from the cup she held. 'I hate it when people think money makes them posh. Luke was always like that, wanting to impress people. Stuff them I say,' she looked around, 'but this does beat lining up at the check in counter though.'

'When Estelle caught Luke cheating, did you give her any money?' I wanted to bring up the divorce, but thought she'd raise it when she was ready.

'We loaned her some from George and my superannuation, but she paid it back within a year, why?'

'All this would have been hard to pull it out of thin air. She had to start somewhere.'

'Estelle once told me she said she would only stay with Luke if it was within her interests to do so. A divorce would have killed his aspirations for a career on the bench, and it's not like he was fit for such a role anyway, but she stayed. Oh, I'm not blind, my daughter would have made sure he paid and she used her time to mix with polite society.' Tears formed in her eyes. She turned to look out the window and, after a few moments, tapped my knee to get my attention. 'She came crying to me once and said he'd made a whore out of her and that she'd make sure it was worth her while.' She looked in her hands. 'That was when I gave her another hundred thousand dollars,' her voice carried the pain of a mother's heartache, 'and I created a monster.'

'No, you loaned your daughter the money to start a business and gain some independence from an unfaithful husband.' I couldn't help smiling, at last there was another person in this world who entertained the fact that Luke Peters was not as he appeared. 'Let's not jump to any conclusions before we hear what Toby Rosen has to say?'

'Tobias Sam, we must refer to him as Tobias.'

Almost on cue the man re-joined us and clipped his seatbelt on. 'We should be down in a few minutes. A car will meet us and take us to the Casino for lunch. Our Adelaide manager has cleared her calendar and will join us in the restaurant.'

Lunch was silver service and for most of the time Rosen directed information at us. Today felt like the murder investigation. I was swamped with information and somewhere amongst the deluge were clues that caused someone to hate Estelle enough to murder her. My phone vibrated in my pocket. Eddie. I excused myself and moved.

'Where are you?'

'Adelaide, why?'

'Well, besides Una on the warpath and looking for you, apparently you're not supposed to leave town without letting them know?'

'Don't worry about that. Did you get that information from Estelle International?'

'Yes.'

'And?'

'And I'm going to need more computing power. We've reached the limit with what we've got, but I did find something interesting. Donna will need to qualify the money side, but the whole business was founded on the porn DVDs. Estelle had found a means to capture the private porn market. I need time, or maybe Tobias Rosen can explain it, but it seems as if just about everyone in Canberra society wanted to star in their own Fifty Shades of Grey movie. How much does Donna know?'

'I don't think it'll be new to her,' I thought of how she'd brought Rosen to attention, 'she's tough enough.'

'Good, none of what I can see between the lines is downright dirty.'

'How much do you need for the computers?'

'Ten grand, maybe more.'

'Come on Eddie, give me a break. You know you never buy new unless you have to so I'm not buying that. Buy more memory if you absolutely have to but no more units because they just won't fit in the front room and I'm not having it take over the entire house.' He remained quiet for once. 'I'll tell you what, get what you need, that's need not want, and use my credit card to pay for it. You know the numbers, but someday soon we're going to have to find a way to justify the investment.'

'I have an idea about that too, but I'll tell you later,' I heard excitement in his voice, 'but it does have to be new stuff this time?'

'Okay, but keep it reasonable, and keep the receipts.'

'No problem, I'll see you both tonight,' I imagined him in the electronics store, it would be like watching a kid in Santa's workshop. Those blue and green eyes flashing everywhere as he agonised over his choices. It was easy to smile, 'and call Una.'

I phoned Una.

'Where are you?'

'Adelaide.'

'Why?'

'Business.'

'How?'

'Jet.'

'What jet?'

'A Cessna Citation picked us up this morning. Donna wanted a meeting with the head of the organisation. He flew in and picked us up.'

'And you're in Adelaide, why?'

'He wants to keep his job is my guess.'

'How is that relevant?'

'Estelle's shares have to go somewhere. Donna is part of the somewhere.'

'And you?'

'I'm the other half.'

'Half of Estelle International?'

'Yeah, half of Estelle's bit anyway.'

'Report to the station when you get back.' I pictured her pacing behind her desk not knowing what to do or say next. 'This is a mess Voss and you're in the middle of it.

'See you tonight.' I could tell she had something she wanted to share. I went back to my lunch.

CHAPTER TWENTY-ONE

The afternoon was more management babble. Rosen extolled the virtues of his management team and the company structure. In all, there were now only four share-holders, Rosen, Donna, me and a separate trust fund set up to manage the superannuation for the models. Donna requested all details of that particular operation to be emailed to her, while he asked for us to approve changes he suggested to re-structure the board now that Estelle had died.

'Definitely not. If that is what all this buttering up has been for Tobias, then you've completely misread the situation. Estelle may have learned a lot from her father, but the hard arse came from me. As I told you earlier, I want a face to face meeting with the complete board, no dissenters, and as soon as we can. But first you will give me full access to the books. Voss and our associate will want complete background information on all personnel, their pay structure, copies of their contracts, you know the sort of thing. Oh, and I want an organisational chart showing everyone, a precis of their job description and your report on why and how each role functions. You can bring it to me on Friday, there's a good lad.'

'I'm...'

'No ifs or buts Mr Rosen, you will not let me down.'

I saw Frank grin at Leon. He turned away to hide it.

'Yes Mrs...?' His embarrassment was evident as he struggled for her name.

'Call me Donna. You can even call me Mum if you want to, Estelle did,' she turned and winked at me, 'do we understand each other Mr Rosen?'

'Perfectly.'

On the way home, the previous tension in the plane had diminished and Donna asked Rosen, 'You said the company held shares in the casino, there are three casinos in the group, right?'

'Yes.'

'And we hold shares in the ownership group?'

'Correct.'

'And the percentage of the total stock?'

'Close to fifteen percent. We, Estelle and I, were negotiating for anther fifteen just before she died.'

'So, the purchase, in cash or kind?'

'Some cash, some shares. Our business is not traded on the stock exchange so the paperwork was going to be troublesome. I've suggested floating the business before, but Estelle was wary of exposing our strategies to the world.'

'And now you have to share with me and Mr Voss, how irksome for you.'

'I must admit, you Donna, are not who I expected?'

'Snap Mr Rosen, Snap.'

Rosen went to the back of the plane and issued orders to Frank and Leon. I watched them put headsets on and assumed they were doing their best to make Donna's wish list happen.

'Wake me when we land please Sam,' she reclined her chair, 'it's been a big day for this little old lady.'

Rosen was back and passed me a scotch. 'Little Old Lady my arse,' he laughed, 'I can see where Estelle got her attitude from.'

'If you reckon she's tough, you should have met George.'

'Frighten you?'

'Nothing frightens me. I was married to Estelle and had them as in-laws,' I smiled at him, 'but they were no match for me.'

'Is that so, Mr Voss?'

'Everyone calls me Voss.' I passed my glass for a refill.

'Even your friends?'

'Especially my friends,' I stared into his eyes, they were the colour of the whisky and about as warm, 'Estelle's murder, have you made a statement as to where you were at the time?'

'What, to the police?'

'Yes, to the police. Where were you when Estelle was murdered?'

'I can't remember.'

'Expect a call from Detective Sergeant Nguyen sometime soon. She's running the case.' For the first time today, I saw something. Maybe it was a wisp of uncertainty that washed across his face. 'I think, three of us in this plane have motive, we all benefited by her death. Now, when you look at a private plane whisking two suspects off interstate for the day well, you can see how a copper's mind works,' his face reminded me of a schoolboy searching for an excuse, 'did you kill Estelle Peters and her husband?

'Shit no, what do you take me for?'

'A man who benefits from the death of another,' I smiled and drained my glass, 'that's all.' I put the glass on the tray and lay my seat back. Donna had the right idea.

Back at the airport, we walked to my car in silence. I opened its door for Donna and waited for her to settle before going to my side. When I sat down I spoke aloud the thoughts that had been running through my head. 'The Estelle I knew had a pretty wild streak in her, but I never figured she would have got a thrill from going down the porn track. Something must have triggered it.'

'I don't know anything other than she broke my heart,' Donna turned away and stared out of her window, 'it's time we were home.'

Una was waiting in her office when I responded to her request to come in to the station. She threw a piece of paper at me, 'Where did you get this list of names?'

'What list of names?' I looked at the sheet of paper I'd scrawled the credits on from Estelle's first movie. 'Where did you get it?'

'I found it under my table. You must have dropped it last night.'

I remembered having it in my pocket. 'Thanks.' I folded it and slipped it into my wallet.

'I had one of the team run those names through the system. Over half of them have diplomatic immunity, but after finding the assistant commissioner, a magistrate, several former government ministers and their wives on that list,' she stared at me, 'I've been heavied into either dropping the case, or to stitch some poor sod up as soon as possible.' She looked around the room. 'And the assistant commissioner wants that sod to be you.'

'So are you going to charge me?'

'With what? You didn't do it.'

I shrugged

'Look Voss, I don't know what you're up to, but I'm not going to bury this. Something's rotten in Saigon and I don't care who smells it. It's better if we find the real murderer and not some sad nobody who's convenient.'

'Got any good news?'

'If you can call it good news, the victim at the Boathouse was an accident.'

'No one gets hit in the neck with the bolt from a crossbow by accident.'

'Apparently, they do. A fourteen-year-old kid broke into his father's gun safe and took the crossbow. He and his mates thought it would be a lark to try and shoot a couple of ducks in flight.' She smiled at me. 'Lucy has had Child Services, a legal team, and the parents in here all day. She's only just left.'

'And you cross referenced them against my list?'

'Be silly not to, wouldn't it?'

'And?'

'Nothing. One of the friends told his dad about the crossbow and the ducks. The father put two and two together and brought the boy in. It was all pretty messy for a while, but the stories stack up. Patrice died as a result of some stupid bloody macho boy's game. It was an accident.'

'Poor Patrice.'

'Now what are we going to do about the other killings?' She turned, lifted her handbag from the rack behind her and put it on the desk.

'Want to share some thoughts over dinner?' I cleared my throat. 'My treat.'

Una closed the lid on her briefcase and slid it under her desk, propping a paperclip under the handle. 'Be nice to know if that's still there in the morning,' she said, 'we'll go in your car.'

CHAPTER TWENTY-TWO

At home, Eddie appeared agitated, but he kept Una company while I changed. The last thing I wanted to do was eat out. He and I had much to discuss, but I wanted to know more about the case and I sensed that Una might be primed to let a few things slip. I stood in the shower, even with water washing over my shoulders, I had a hundred thoughts buzzing around in my head. This case had been like that from the moment Lucy and I had walked into the Peters' place.

So, at this point, what did I know?

The security system provided nothing and information Eddie had discovered about their movements showed they were creatures of habit. The perpetrator could have understood their routine.

The way Luke Peters had been tortured and killed suggested the killer wanted something, but what was it they wanted to know?

I started to draw lines on the fogged-up glass. This was getting to be a habit.

The killer had to have assumed Tamsyn, Luke Peter's secretary, had known something, and did giving it to him get her killed?

Instinct told me the killer was male.

Tamsyn's information had led him to Rory and the chauffer. By discounting Patrice, we could surmise the killer had an issue with Estelle.

He didn't know the woman had contempt for her husband, that watching his torture hadn't fazed her. She may have even enjoyed it.

This was all about Estelle, but whether it had been revenge, jealousy or spite I had yet to find out.

I needed Eddie to narrow his parameters, our search was too wide

Donna arrived while I was showering and, from my bedroom door, I could see Eddie had command of the kitchen while she sat at the table reading reams of financial guff that Rosen had emailed through. I slipped in to the lounge room and left a note for Eddie, asking him to remove everyone from the search except Luke Peters, Estelle and Tamsyn. He needed to scan every newspaper article, social media outlet or calls to and from their phones, only adding in the chauffer and Adderton when a link came up. We had to forget the film set, Peter Peters, and the business deals he and Estelle shared. Peters was not on my suspect list. I closed the door and went to the kitchen.

Una slid off her stool as I walked through the door, 'Eddie was telling me about his life on the outside, an interesting tale, but how much does he know about you, Voss?'

'Enough to be able to call me Sam sometimes and get away with it.'

'Have you told him about how you got your name and why you became a copper?' She picked up her bag.

'Why would I? It's irrelevant.' I started to feel annoyed with her silly games, always trying to create suspicion between people.

'Come on, Sam,' She laboured on my name and it grated with me. She smiled at Eddie, 'ask him some time, it's a great yarn.' She closed with a wink.

'Like I said, it's not worth the chat.' I put my hand in the middle of her back and guided her out to the car. Stepping into the garage she slipped and nearly fell, I steadied her until she regained her balance, I should have asked if she was okay, but I didn't care. She had always worn heels high enough to put her at eye level with most of the men under her command. I'd always figured it was a ploy to either dominate or intimidate. If she had pain she didn't let on. I held the door for her. We'd known each other for a long time and had shared more experiences than most long married couples, but tonight it hit me for the first time how far apart we'd grown. I really didn't know her anymore and I wasn't sure I even liked her.

As we backed out of the drive I said. 'You say you need help. I can give you some advice, that's all.'

'It can't be anything more.' I could hear neither pride nor pain in her voice.

'Cut your list down. Estelle wouldn't talk, Tamsyn did, and two more people died. Luke Peters was collateral damage.'

'I can see it took a bit for you to admit that.' Her face was expressionless. 'So who do we eliminate?'

'You need to look at what the first three victims had in common with Adderton and the chauffer.'

'That's a pile of work. I haven't got enough people to go through all of Estelle's contacts to see if and when they've used a hire car?'

'I'm not suggesting you have and it will take a lot of time, but it's what I'd do next. Think about it, you haven't had anyone murdered since the chauffer, maybe it was him they wanted. Go back to the beginning and start from there.'

'As easy as that?'

'Yep.' The traffic was light and we glided through the city. 'If it's too hard to do, Eddie bought a new computer today, I could ask him to feed in your data and do a bit of analysis for you.'

'Pro Bono?'

'No, he'd need to be paid. He has to pay off that computer somehow.'

'You financed it, didn't you?'

'What can I say? You all think I'm an easy touch anyway.'

'Our files are confidential and if it did show up a link, I don't want you racing in and buggering up my investigation.'

'He could work with your team if you wanted.'

'That'd be like having you looking over my shoulder. No thank you.'

Okay, but don't say I didn't make an offer.' I flashed a grin at her and looked back at the road.

'Let me think on it,' she said, and leant forward to rub her ankle, 'at least until after I've eaten.'

CHAPTER TWENTY-THREE

I felt the bed shake, rolled over to look at the clock and saw Donna sitting with her back against the head board, a piece of toast in one hand and a cup of tea in the other.

'What time is it?'

'Ever asked yourself what happened to Luke's first wife, or wonder who she was?'

'No. What time is it?'

She held the toast in her mouth and steadied herself with the free hand and twisted to look at the clock. 'Quarter to five. I couldn't sleep and I've worried myself sick about all of this. Then I got to wondering. Luke was a good ten years older than Estelle and he'd been married before. If his first wife had known he was a root rat, then did she divorce him and where is she now? If she'd died and he was a widower what happened to her?'

'Donna, you might be a genius,' I threw the covers back and slid out of bed. It wasn't until I reached the en-suite that I realised I was naked, 'sorry,' I whispered through the crack of the sliding door.

'Wait till I tell the girls at the bridge club I was in bed with a naked man.'

'I was in bed and you were on top of it. That's how it was and don't ever do it again, okay?'

'Better if I tell them my way.'

'Wake Eddie while I get dressed and see if you can find her. Births, deaths marriages etcetera.'

The door slid open. I turned away from her and faced the wall.

'Water won't hide much,' she said, 'if you hadn't been so quick to rush in here, I could have told you that her name is Stacey. She's still using his surname and lives in Perth. I phoned her last night and she's expecting to receive us this afternoon.'

I turned to look at her over my shoulder. 'We haven't got time to get tickets and be in Western Australia today,' I felt a twinge in my neck from twisting too far. Old age was creeping up on me. 'Now get out of here, please?'

'Better hurry, our plane will be here in an hour.'

'Our plane. What plane?'

'The Estelle, the one we flew in yesterday. Tobias was reluctant at first, but I reminded him about the size of our shareholding. He was ever so obliging after that. Come on let's use this fortune to do some good.'

Eddie was in the kitchen when I sat down to breakfast, poached eggs and bacon. 'This is exciting,' he said, 'I haven't been to Perth for years.'

Donna sat beside me. 'Last night, after Eddie got your note, we started talking and I suggested that he come with us, we can work on the plane and he said he can tap into VU-3 from the air.' She smiled at me and continued. 'It's a bit like being in a scene from Miss Marple.

'So it's settled then, and you had this planned last night?' I asked.

'Yep.' Eddie sounded too pleased with himself.'

'Tobias needed to be notified with enough time to organise the plane, so we had to do it last night,' Donna said, 'and you were with the competition. It'd be unwise for Una to know what's going on now, wouldn't it?'

Eddie put a cup of coffee in front of me and sat down to his eggs. 'I think this all goes back a long way,' he said, 'whatever happened has been dormant until the killer was ready or had enough information to make sure they got the right person. And I don't think it was Estelle, Luke, or Tamsyn. I think there's one more person who they have to kill to satisfy their need for vengeance. Others may have to die before he or she gets them, but the target is still out there.'

I pointed my knife at him. Donna tutted and I put it down. 'And you base this on what?'

'The data. I can't find a strong enough link to make someone want to commit a murder,' I went to interject and he held his hand up to stop me, 'I put in all the known psychological parameters.'

'Do I need to ask?' I said

'No need to fear, Uncle Eddie's here. I asked Gabby and she suggested the internet. That led me to an associate at the Uni who introduced me to the right woman. I told her I was trying to develop a programme to profile killers. She was most helpful.'

'You two can talk on the plane. We have to meet it in half an hour. That car of yours still got a siren?'

'No.'

'Pity, it'd help us run a few lights if we need to.' I was sure Donna was winding me up, but the little old lady who needed protecting was proving every bit as formidable as the first day I met her.

Estelle International had a Perth office and the manager had arranged a car and driver to meet our plane. Stacey Peters was a woman in her early fifties and not as I'd imagined. I'd expected a woman with greying hair and matronly. Stacey was everything but that. If Estelle had lived another ten years, this is how she might have looked. Luke Peters liked fine drawn blondes with a veneer of class.

'I wondered if someone from the police would call when I read about Luke and Estelle's deaths, but no-one did.' she turned to Donna, 'I'm glad you called last night, I haven't known if I should phone, or what to do. I'm sorry she died, I'm going to miss her.'

'Why?' I had a million things fighting for space in my mind.

'We had a lot in common, Estelle and I.' She waved for us to sit down. 'You see, after Luke and I married, I found out about his little perversions.'

'Perversions? What do you mean?' Donna was ready for this woman to open up and so I decided to let her take the lead. 'That sounds horrible.'

'It was. At first I thought he was gay or weird. When he brought the first man home he said it was because he wanted to share me. I was young and stupid and it was fun for a while. Every other night we'd smoke pot get naked and three of us would romp around, although it was always a different man. One night Luke said he wanted to film us with a video camera.'

'No...' Donna let the word hang there.'

'This man was older and I think he was in business, married, or connected to crime. I never knew his name. He slapped me hard across the face and started raving about being caught in a honey trap,' she made quotation marks with her fingers, 'Luke stood back and pleaded that it wasn't.' I thought Luke was my protector, someone who would rescue me if anything happened, but that wasn't him. He stood back and watched, helped himself off while this man raped, beat and sodomised me. Luke Peters is,' she corrected herself, 'was, a despicable human being who ruined my life. I've felt ashamed for years.'

Donna shifted along the sofa and held Stacey's hand. 'It's okay love, being assaulted is nothing to be ashamed of.'

'I know. I knew it then,' she began to sob and then pulled it together. 'Luke was charming, but underneath he was just a slimy excuse for a man. I'm not ashamed of what was done to me. I'm ashamed of not speaking up.'

'You can let it all out now, we're not going to divulge any secrets.' Donna was allowing this woman time to tell her story. 'Do you want the men to leave?'

'No, it's fine, they have to hear everything I know.'

'But how did you cope?' Donna was still leading the conversation.

'I asked for a divorce and left.'

'That quick, eh?' I wished I'd left it to Donna to ask the questions, but it was too late, I'd said it now.

'Well not really, for a long time it had been getting rough and stopped being fun for me. I kept wondering what my mother would think, or what would happen later, if our children ever found out.'

'Children?' I looked around the living room, the place was devoid of family photos.

'I found the right man in Jesus, no children in that. After the divorce, I joined the order,' she held up a little cross that hung from a chain around her neck, 'it helped mum understand my divorce. I kept the secret about my marriage until she died. I left the order after that. That's when Estelle found me, and I told her everything.'

'She knew?' I'd promised myself to hold back, but the copper in me pushed the question out.

'Yes. I think it might have happened to her, too. She didn't say, but I'm sure she knew something about what happened to me.'

Donna shot me a look as if warning me to shut up and asked. 'How long ago was that?'

'A few years ago now. She'd been married ten years and found me with the Nuns a couple of years later, so yeah, four years ago. I wasn't sure of her at first, but it ended up a nice day. We talked about our lives before Luke, our aspirations, you know? A good marriage to the right man, kids. I'd have grandchildren now if my dreams had worked out,' her face seemed to turn grey as she turned to look at the ceiling, 'but it wasn't to be.'

'No grandchildren for me either.' Donna said and patted Stacey's hand.

Her eyes vacant, Stacey appeared to look for something beyond the window. After a moment she drew her hands away and turned back to Donna. 'Like I said, he was a creep and I'm certainly glad Luke Peters hadn't fathered any children with me.'

CHAPTER TWENTY-FOUR

I turned my phone on when we reached the car. The driver held the door for Donna, asking if she wished to call into the office.

'Not today thank you,' she looked at his name tag, 'Azar, it's a long flight home, take us to the plane please.'

'Certainly, Mrs...?'

Donna didn't give him her name.

Eddie slid into the rear seat on the other side of the car while I rode up front with Azar.

'Did you drive Mr And Mrs Peters often?' I tried to sound casual. I knew my questioning technique could sometimes intimidate and that's not what I wanted today.

'Mr Peters no, I never saw him. Mrs Peters yes, but only twice. Mr Tobias was who I waited on most. All business, Mr Tobias.' His voice was pure venom.

'You don't like him?'

He stared at the road as he considered his answer. 'Let's just say he's a very cold man.'

'I'm with you. I met him yesterday and thought he liked being in control too much. Mrs Peters' mother reminded him that the company wasn't all his. It seemed to work.'

'I should buy shares then.' He laughed.

In the back seat, Eddie was working on his computer and Donna was gazing out the window.

'Did Mrs Peters ever go anywhere other than the office?' I asked.

'Only the office and a few weeks ago she went to see the lady where we went today. She sometimes used her personal car too.'

'That's it?'

'Yes Mr Voss, that's it.'

I hadn't considered that Donna might have wanted grandchildren. She and George had never mentioned it when Estelle and I were together. A million things fought for space in my mind and I supposed it was natural for Donna to wonder about what might have been. Eddie was humming something familiar while he worked, I decided to follow Donna's lead and stare into the streetscape as we passed.

The flight home was quiet with all of us either napping, or looking out the window. More than once I scratched my head and wondered at the way life twists and turns. I never thought I'd have a personal jet at my service, but today it seemed we did and I was in it. My phone beeped a message. Lucy wanted to talk with me as soon as possible and asked me to text her with a time. Then she sent a second message that just said, *"Goss"*. I was intrigued. Who the hell was Goss? I rifled through all the names in my memory and came up with nothing. Donna didn't know anyone called Goss, neither did Eddie, but he googled it anyway and came up with nothing.

Lucy arrived as dinner was cooking with Gabby trailing her in. It seems Eddie had decided to invite her too. Donna went off to have a shower and a lie-down, asking to be called when dinner was ready. Gabby offered to help in the kitchen and Lucy and I moved outside to the patio, facing each other over a glass table.

'Who's Goss?'

'What?'

'You heard me. Who's Goss?'

I could see she was starting to crack up, a slow shaking of the shoulders as her mirth squeezed between her teeth in a whistled laugh. 'Jeeze, I hope you haven't been wasting your time searching every Goss in the phone book,' she peered at me through her almost hysteria, 'you have, haven't you?'

'Not me, no.'

'Eddie then? You didn't send him on a quest to find someone who doesn't exist.' She took a minute to contain herself. 'Goss is gossip, not a person.'

'Okay, you got me,' I tried to deadpan the situation, but I knew it would get back to the station, 'so what's the goss?'

'That list of names you gave Una to check for any one being blackmailed, well they're a kind of swingers group, a sex party set. The warehouse is just a venue for everyone to,' she made quotation marks in the air, 'get it on. The way she lingered on the last word made me cringe.

'So you can scratch that lot off the list then?'

'I can't say, you know that. Anyway, what are you doing flying around in a private plane? Is there something you want to tell me about your flight to Perth today?'

'Nope.'

'So a joy flight to Adelaide yesterday and another to Perth today. How are you able to afford it? And I'm not blind to what's happening in your lounge room. All that equipment has had to come from somewhere and I don't think Eddie's exactly rolling in it. You're on a copper's salary and the job doesn't pay that well?'

'Maybe Donna needed cheering up and we used her cash. It's not relevant to your investigation Sergeant.'

'Look Voss, this is still a murder investigation and you're a serving officer who has been considered either a suspect or implicated in the case. You let me know where you're going at all times, got it.' I could see she was annoyed and decided to push a couple of buttons.

'Did you want to come with me?' I smiled.

'No, I didn't want to come,' the smile didn't work, 'where were you yesterday and today?'

'Donna and I were looking at parts of our inheritance. Tobias Rosen the CEO owns ten percent of the company, Donna forty, and my share is equal to hers. I'm having trouble adjusting to it all, but I'll cope.'

'Forty percent of what exactly?'

'Estelle International. It seems that leaving me was profitable for Estelle, if not all that safe.'

'This Tobias Rosen, does he have a motive?'

'I don't know, but I was going to ask you to check him out. However, I don't think he's the type. Soft hands.'

'Anything else you should tell me?'

'Patrice, the girl who was killed by the arrow, was she supposed to be at the swinger's thing? And her friends, were they there?'

'Who were her friends?'

I felt in the pocket of my jacket. The card I'd meant to give Una was still there. With Donna running us all over the continent, I'd forgotten about it. 'This is one of their cards,' I read the name and passed it to Lucy, 'She certainly didn't call herself that. The other girl called her Steph, must be short for Stephanie.'

'Shit Voss, it's just like you to withhold information. Just what are you playing at?'

'Ease up Tiger. I'm sorry, it may not be relevant anyway.'

'Relevant. Look at the web address on the card.' She thrust it at me and tapped the words at the bottom. I squinted. 'Oh for heaven's sake, when are you getting your eyes tested? The website is for Xirena Zelazny Modelling, that's where we went on the first day, to the fashion house. Laurelle was the sales lady who called herself the manager. The business is a front for prostitution.'

She dialled the number and I could only hear part of the conversation, but it seemed as if Lucy was booking a couple of girls. She asked for Stephanie and Julie and then said it was for Mr and Mrs Richard Stirling, and named a hotel. 'Eight o'clock tomorrow, yes you have our card details on file,' she flapped around in her hand bag, 'no, look I can't remember it and I had it written on a piece of paper, too.' She waited. 'No, I don't want to call my husband. It's an early birthday surprise you see.' She paused again, her back was to me and as much as I wanted to break into the conversation, I held my tongue, 'I could ring poor Estelle or Patrice, but...' Lucy was fake sobbing, 'you can, thank you, Laurelle, isn't it?' Still with the phone to her ear she asked, 'Have you anything in your specialty department that might drive him wild?' Another pause, 'oh good, I'll come in tomorrow and you can show me.' Lucy stayed on the phone for a couple of seconds then turned it off.

'Someone has a date for tomorrow night,' she said.

'You used the assistant commissioner's name.'

'The only one I could remember from the swinger's club.'

'What, Richard Stirling has been there?'

'It's from him that Una's getting all the pressure. It seems our good and great Assistant Commissioner and his friends star in their own kinky movies, but let's hear what the girls say first, eh?'

'Why not just drag them in and question them?'

'This might be more fun. I'll need to clear it with Una, but are you or Eddie flying anywhere tomorrow?'

'No plans at present, why?'

'Una told me to tell you to stay put, that's all. Seems our Assistant Commissioner is getting worried about his little hobby being discovered.'

'And he's putting the squeeze on her?'

'Not only him. This club is a who's who of Canberra.'

'Is Peter Peters in it?'

'Yep, why?'

'Just wondered?' I smiled again, 'I wonder if he'd leak anything to the press?'

'You never know, stranger things have happened.' She said, passing me the business card. I looked at the photo, it was Laurelle, but the name was Sheena. In her position, I wouldn't want anyone to know my real name either.

Eddie called to let us know dinner was ready. I was starving and ushered Lucy to her chair.

CHAPTER TWENTY-FIVE

Alone in the kitchen, Eddie and Donna approached me using a pincer like ambush movement. 'What are you two conspiring?' Something was up but just what it was I wasn't sure.

'What do you think of Tobias?' Donna asked.

'Just another suit.'

'Might be more than that,' Eddie said, 'VU-3 has found some stuff you should know about.' He waved for us to follow him into the lounge room. As I stood up, my phone vibrated. No surprise there, it was Una.

'I'm sending a taxi for you,' her words were firm, not angry. I put the phone on speaker, the others stayed quiet and Donna wrote shorthand notes into the legal pad she'd started carrying, 'I have information I need to discuss. I can't do it at work and I can't be seen with you. Uber have a driver coming in ten minutes, I'll text you his number if you want to track his progress.'

'Can you talk?'

'No and I'm not in a position to tell you where I am yet, but phone me when you're in the car and I'll tell you where to send the driver.' It took a moment to realise Una was whispering.

'Can you tell me where you are?'

'I'm safe for now, but I can't risk any of the team overhearing, I wouldn't ask, but...'

'...you need a knight in shining armour.' I finished her sentence for her.

'Something like that.'

'Don't worry about Uber, I'll find you.' I motioned to Eddie to start tracking.

'What if they've got you staked out?'

Keeping my eyes on Eddie as he typed, I said, 'They won't. I'll work on a hunch.'

He passed me the address. 'Stay low, I have a secret weapon.'

Eddie was scanning the security cameras in the homes that surrounded the blocks around my house. 'No one's watching,' he said, 'what's the plan?'

'Donna's going to take the Cooper S out for another drive. I may as well use it now I'd gone to the expense of getting a roadworthy and re-registering it. I'm going to crouch in the back with a blanket over me with a couple of cushions on top. We'll pick up Una, find out what's frightened her and bring her here.'

'Better still, we could say we're going to check on my place and you can sit in the front like a normal person,' Donna scoffed, 'hide in the back like a kid? Don't be ridiculous.'

'You know what's up, don't you?' Eddie asked.

"I have a hunch, that's all.'

'Spill the beans mister.' Donna was starting to sound like Ma Baker.

'I think the police raid on the little sex club gathering last night has her frightened.'

'Why should that concern her?'

'The Assistant Commissioner and his wife were sprung.' I shrugged and scrambled for something to say that wouldn't seem trite. 'Una must know something he doesn't want to surface.'

'What about the rest of your team?'

'Let's get Una first and then, if you can get a message to Gabby and Lucy, think up something to get them to come here.'

Eddie passed me the address. Una was in the lobby of Rydges Hotel.

In the end, I decided against the subterfuge. 'We'll take the Ford,' I said, and went to the closet to open the gun safe. I'd kept a few range pistols from my gun club days and picked up a long barrel 44 Magnum. Being a Clint Eastwood fan, I always wanted to be like Dirty Harry, and this was the first pistol I'd bought when I joined the club. I put it back and took out a small revolver I could keep in my jacket and the Glock I bought two years ago. I loaded them and threw Donna the keys.

'I'm still driving?'

'Do your worst, but remember this thing is heavier and has more power than the Cooper.'

The drive was uneventful. Una was in a dark corner of the lounge with the concierge. In front of her, she had a tall glass filled with ice and something that looked like scotch. I lifted and smelt it. 'Iced tea, good girl,' I said, 'but who, or what is scaring you?'

The concierge went to move, she patted the seat for him to stay. 'I'll need you to stay now my friends are here,' she said. 'The girls in three-o-five. Not a lucky number. All three of them are dead.'

'How did you find them?'

'The desk sergeant told me you took one of the girls, Julie, home the other day. I came to ask why and this is what I find. Mark here says he saw a tall, older man coming from the room this afternoon. I showed him some photos and this is who he identified.'

I looked at her phone. 'Richard Stirling?'

'Spot on, now because you were here and because you are, via Estelle, linked to the other murders, I reckon he's going to try and pin this on you.'

'Me?'

'He's done a little tidying up after last night, I think.' She felt my pocket. 'Want to give me the Glock?'

'No.'

'Want to see the room?'

'No. You have photos?' I thought she'd have documented everything.

'Yes.'

'Let's get out of here then.'

'What about Mark here?'

'He comes with us.'

Donna had parked in the emergency services spot. It was a short walk and we didn't waste time. Donna knew what to do and wound her way through a few back streets, until we were well clear of the hotel.

Mark was a mess, understandable after what he'd seen, and knowing the identity of the killer, he was frightened for his family.

I remembered Laurelle. 'Who can you trust?' I said to Una.

'Why?'

'The working girls' contact is the woman from the fashion house. Her name's Laurelle,' I started to think on the run. 'Don't worry, I'll call Eddie.'

I spent a couple of minutes on the phone. Eddie had messaged me the address while I asked him to sift through the security footage from the hotel. Donna squealed the tyres as she handbrake-turned across the median strip and toward Laurelle's place. Time was in short supply.

I'm sure Laurelle expected no one to call. I pounded on her door until it opened, one eye peering through a mud mask. 'Remember me, Detective Voss, I need you to come with me.' I could smell the cucumber she would have placed on her eyelids.

'I'm not dressed,' she looked at the street.

My arm was on her elbow, I steered her toward the car and Una pushed the door open. 'I'll bring you back once you're safe.'

'What do you mean safe?'

Una pulled her in and clipped her belt on for her, 'Julie, Steph and Leah are dead, murdered.'

'I just booked them for a client, less than two hours ago, Mrs Stirling phoned.' Laurelle said.

'Mrs Stirling won't be keeping the appointment, the caller was one of ours.' I searched for the right thing to say. 'Sorry, it was one of Superintendent Knight's officers who made that call.'

'Why?'

'She wanted to confirm the connection.'

Laurelle dropped her head in her hands and cried. 'I'm ruined, ruined.' she repeated until it became a chant.

I asked Una to call Lucy and anyone from the team who she knew might be in danger and tell them to meet at my place. Somewhat surprised she acquiesced without protest. I called Eddie and told him to shut all the computers down immediately. He offered up a token argument but knew by my voice tone to do as I asked.

At home, I ushered Lucy and Una out to the patio. Eddie threw some nibbles together to sustain us while we debriefed. My gut told me the Assistant Commissioner was the women's killer, but I wanted the others to be sure. Una showed Lucy the pictures and passed her the statement from Mark.

Lucy passed it back. 'We have him then?' I almost thought I saw her smile. 'It's him isn't it, Super?'

'But why kill everyone, it doesn't make any sense.' Una said.

I stayed quiet and listened while they analysed and planned. They were frightened. If they couldn't trust their Assistant Commissioner, who could they trust? I left them to it and joined Eddie inside. I could see he had something on his mind.

CHAPTER TWENTY-SIX

It was hard to find humour in the situation, but inside I was almost smirking. By calling me Una had reinforced the fact they were not such a crack homicide team without me. Under other circumstances, now would be the time to gloat and I did want that moment to redeem myself after the humiliation of suspension, but now was not appropriate. I sat with Una and Lucy as they planned their strategy. Arresting an Assistant Commissioner would be difficult. Thankfully Eddie had pulled a few stills from the hotel security system and those monitoring the coming and going of the film set carpark to back up what we suspected. He'd called up the booking log from the limo company to confirm the time they'd be picking up him and his wife. Security vision from their home added to the evidence.

'How?' Una stumbled for words, 'how did you get these photos and this data so quickly.

'If I tell you, I shall need to kill you,' Eddie used his best imitation of a KGB operative.

'You know I can't use any of this as evidence. What about people's privacy?' Una sounded exhausted.

'You don't have time,' I was rushing her, 'get the hotel secured. Lucy, you need to meet forensics in that hotel room now.'

Una had her mojo back, 'Lucy, the concierge, Mark, called it in, so we have his statement. Go now and I'll catch up with you at the station. The hotel's sealed the room until forensics get there, I've told them not to hand any vision of the passages or grounds to anyone but you.'

'You okay, Ma-am?' Lucy put her hand out to comfort her superior. Una turned away. 'I am now. I just needed some space to think.' She smiled, winked at me and turned back to Lucy. 'Go, and do everything by the book now, we don't want this one slipping away.'

Lucy disappeared into the dark.

'Want to sit in while I interview Laurelle?' Una asked.

'Yes, but we both know that would cloud already muddied waters. You're on your own from now on.'

'But you won't mind seeing the Assistant Commissioner fall either.'

'That's why I'm staying out of it.'

'The bastard has murdered... what is it now?' She used her fingers to count, 'seven people, maybe more.'

I wanted to tell her there were only three, that only the girls in the hotel had been his victims, but I'd leave it for her to work out.

'Okay if I take your car?' she asked.

'Sure, take the bugging device out of it too while you are at it,' I tried for the cheesiest grin I could manage, 'but come with me, there's something I need to show you first.'

I led her toward the lounge room, 'I want you to meet someone.'

'Someone?'

'VU-3 is mine,' Eddie stood between us and the door, 'and I don't share my toys.'

'It'll be okay, mate.'

'Not tonight it won't. I have its guts all over the floor and if anyone moves a wire or trips over a diode then it could blow the whole thing up. It's almost perfect, but one wrong wire or a simple short caused by a clumsy foot and

I'll end up with Frankenstein's Monster rather than Brad Pitt. So, who's it going to be Una, Frankie or Brad?'

'It's been so long, I'm probably better suited to Frankie, but if Brad's on offer, just call me when he's ready.'

Una asked if we could babysit Laurelle until someone from the station could pick her up. She called Mark to go into the station with her and confirm his report. Una knew to be careful; charging a superior of murder was not something she'd done before.

Convicting the assistant commissioner was paramount and as I walked them to the car. 'You know you can only charge him for the hotel murders now,' I said.

'What, and let him walk on the rest?' The way she delivered her whisper could've scorched paint.

'I don't think it was him, or her for that matter, just get him cold for the girls. I'll think about the others and let you know,' I said.

'You look after Laurelle until I send a car, okay'

'Okay.'

'And no tricks. I know how you work, Voss.'

She must have been reading my mind. 'No tricks.'

She cocked an eyebrow.

'Ma-am.' I said.

Laurelle had removed the facemask and was sitting across the table from Donna, rolling a cup of coffee between her palms. I made myself a cup, offered the women a refill and found some biscuits in the pantry and cheese from the fridge to go with it. Donna would have used a special platter for such occasions, tonight a dinner plate had to do the job. I put them in the middle of the table. I grabbed a bottle of scotch, put some ice in a pair of tumblers and set them down in front of the women.

Eddie must have heard the ice or smelt the whisky, because he morphed into the room, slipped in behind me and filled another tumbler. 'If we're having a party,' he said, 'I'd hate to miss it.' He sat by Laurelle and moved my coffee across the table.

Donna had made notes on her legal pad and I put my phone on the table and set it ready to record. I could see Laurelle's eyes fixed on it and it seemed to unsettle her.

'I'll put it away,' I said.'

She waved her hand to indicate she was happy to have it record our conversation.

'We spoke with a woman in Western Australia today,' Laurelle stared at the ice in her glass while I spoke. I poured more whisky and passed the bottle to Donna. Eddie's eyes followed it, like a dog's after a sausage, 'you may have heard of her, Stacey, Luke's ex-wife.'

'I know who she is. Why?' Laurelle sculled the whisky and looked at Eddie to refill her glass.

'Something got Estelle and Luke killed. All these murders started there. Any idea what might have triggered that?'

'I don't know what you're talking about. I'm just the manager of a dress shop.'

I slapped the table, Laurelle and Donna jumped, Eddie steadied the whisky. 'And I'm Saint Peter. Look, you can either pretend all of this is a dream, or you can help. If you help, I'll protect you, but if you'd sooner take your chances at home, I'll take you back there. One thing's for sure, the bloke who killed Julie,' I slapped the table again, 'also shot Leah,' I slapped the table for the third time, and Laurelle jumped, 'and blew Steph's brains all over the room.' I raised my hand again then let it drop. She was quivering.

'Enough,' Donna said, 'you're frightening the lady. Shame on you, Sam. It's okay, Laurelle, we just want to know what you know so we can keep you safe.' She gave me a wink, 'I'll keep the bad old detective on his leash.'

It took a minute or two before Laurelle sat up and laughed. 'The number of times I've heard that on the phone when someone asked for a dungeon, a dominatrix. Yes, Estelle had interests in fashion houses, however she also provided venues equipment and instructors for elite clients.'

'I want to know if any of these clients went rogue, did anyone ever go over the top?' I allowed some exasperation into my voice.

'We weren't that kind of service.'

'Look dear, we only want to know the truth, I think what Sam is trying to ask, did anyone die on the job as a result of an equipment failure or something.' Donna asked.

'No, nothing like that. My branch was faultless, the books tallied. I met the KPI's every month, for both the shop and the venues. I did my job and kept everything in order.'

'Okay, let's try it another way,' I said, 'what about young Tamsyn, how did she fit in the picture? Was she one of your girls?'

'No, I think Luke may have made some private movies with her, but he only rented the place when he had a new woman, well not a woman really. I doubt if his type were ever over twenty, even younger by my guess.'

'So, who hired the venue?'

It was only Laurelle and me talking now. I felt the table rock when Eddie went to say something and Donna squeezed down enough to reach him with her foot. By the look on his face she used more force than he expected.

'I have a list.'

181

'At home, or the shop?' My mind raced, the only car I had was the Mini and I hated driving it.

'Here,' she said, and removed a chain from around her neck. She opened the locket and took out a small memory card. 'It holds a lot of information for such a small thing,' she made quotation marks with her fingers, 'Estelle didn't want it to fall into the wrong hands.'

Everyone was using the same gesture lately and it annoyed me. Too much TV I thought.

Laurelle continued, 'she said if anything ever happened to her not to give it to Luke, Rosen, or anyone from the business, only you, Mr Voss.'

'You could have done that when my sergeant and I called after her murder.'

'That's true, but I was flustered.'

I slapped the table again. 'Or you thought you might be able to use it as leverage against someone.' I passed the card to Eddie.

'I'll check it.' he said and stood up. Donna followed him.

CHAPTER TWENTY-SEVEN

I needed somewhere to think. The shower was somewhere I wouldn't be interrupted, but with everyone moving around and Una's troops likely to show up to collect Laurelle, that wasn't an option.

'Here,' Eddie passed me the memory card.

'Thanks,' I dropped the card into my saucer and passed the locket back to Laurelle. 'Put it on,' I said, as I sloshed some whisky over the card. I pushed it onto a tissue with the back of my finger nail and asked Laurelle to dry it and put it back.

'No prints?' she asked.

'Something like that, yeah.'

'Trying to protect you lot here I guess,' she grinned knowingly. I didn't respond, 'and if the police ask for it?'

'Give it to them,' I said.

'You sure? There's a lot of incriminating stuff on there.'

'I don't think it will worry Estelle.' Donna said.

'Well no, but it might embarrass some powerful people.'

'Does it embarrass you?' Donna asked.

'Yes, it does, I got caught up in this because I'd sold my business to Estelle and wanted a job. I didn't sign up to become the madam of a high-class hooker shop.' She trembled as she spoke. 'I should've said no, but the girls were young and innocent. I thought I might be able to steer them away from it.'

'But you couldn't?' Donna asked.

'They liked the money too much. After struggling to get modelling work most of them were hardly able to clothe themselves, especially with the kind of outfits they needed to make an impression.'

'How did you recruit, dear?' Donna showed her gentle side.

'We ran several workshops a year, and not just in Australia, either. Estelle used the same business model for our overseas markets too. The interest just mushroomed. You'd be surprised how many young and impressionable girls would come to Estelle International with dreams of becoming the next big thing in modelling. Sometimes Estelle would sit in our back office and cry whenever a mother brought a girl not quite in her teens in to try out for an audition. She would say we were robbing them of their childhood.'

'Did this happen often?'

'The girls?' Laurelle sounded tired.

'No, my daughter crying. As a mother I'd like to know.'

'Oh yeah, I see. Not often, as much as she could show a soft side to me, she was tough on the girls. If they could get through the first week, they had a chance of making it. A lot of them made it through the first week, but not many made the big time.'

'And that's how Julie and her friends ended up as escorts?' I asked.

'Yes. This is a powerful city with powerful visitors from all over the world. Some of these visitors have special cravings and that's where we came in. Canberra was the first office of her empire, but now we have branches in over thirty countries.'

I was trying to get my head around the numbers. No wonder Estelle needed to use a Cayman Islands bank account. The germ of an idea was fighting to find space in my mind for an international hit man to be involved. I squashed it as fast as it came. A hit man would have flown in, taken his shot and flown out. Those cuts on Luke kept telling me the killer wanted something and it was personal.

'Tell me how it worked, every step, name names, I don't care, I just want to find who killed them. Say I'm a girl of...'

'Fourteen, 'she said.

'Younger than I expected, but let's say she is fourteen, I want to know everything from start until she is too old to work anymore.'

'They never stop. It's horrible to see, but we did at least make sure they contributed a portion of their earnings into superannuation accounts.'

I checked my phone and put it back on the table. 'Now this is just for us, but I want you to understand it's important not to deviate or embellish the truth. I can't read you your rights or anything because I'm suspended, but anything you do say will help keep you safe.

'I know, I watch the detective shows on television, I never thought for one minute I'd end up in a similar situation.

For the next twenty minutes she described the way the Estelle International modelling agencies worked, what happened if the girls and boys failed at any step and the paths they could take. She quoted names that even I knew. Estelle had managed to weave her way into every aspect of film, television, fashion and modelling industries, they were all there. Tobias Rosen had his soft little fingers in things too. Reading between the lines, he was the architect of their pathway to prostitution. However, that was not where a murderer would come from.

'Did anyone hold a grudge? You know, a mother getting pissed because her child didn't make it. Maybe a boyfriend finding out the woman he wanted as a wife was screwing for money?' I liked the sound my hand made when I hit the table, but Laurelle was talking anyway.

'No, not that I can think of.'

'Did you tell the parents and the girls,' I checked myself, 'and boys, this is how it could pan out?'

'Kind of.'

'What do you mean kind of?' This time I did slap the table again, Donna did her comfort thing, but I could see she was beginning to get frustrated as well.

'We had nothing written in the contract. Rosen made sure there was nothing that could harm the company in our documentation. Once the girls were trained, we had them stay in a house or a hotel in a city for a few days, where we would hold a welcome dinner. Estelle would start her speech with her famous quote.'

'And what was that dear?' Donna was starting to sound like syrup.

Laurelle straightened her shoulders. 'Many of you seated here tonight are looking for something you may or may not find. Hard work and dedication will be a big part of it, but there is more to success than that. Yes, luck plays a part too, but so does desperation. I found out long ago that...' she looked at me and I saw tears beginning to fill her eyes, I nearly felt sorry for the woman, but I hardened against it, '...to find your prince, you have to kiss a lot of frogs, but along the road to finding the right frog, you'll end up kissing a lot of toads first.' She slumped again and turned to Donna, 'I'm still working my way through the toads myself. Even I have fallen into the trap of providing a private service.'

'We're not here to judge or comment on how you live your life,' I said, 'I just want to find the killer or killers.

It's what I do and I'm bloody good at it.' I lifted her chin so she could see my eyes, 'I want you to think. Did anyone go out on a job and not come home?'

'I don't think so. All our models had escorts, we used a limousine company to ferry either the client or the model.'

'E P Limousines?' I asked.

'They're one of Estelle's companies.'

'And the drivers knew what the models were doing?'

'Always, Estelle paid them well and they did as they were asked. Everyone signed confidentiality agreements.'

'Did they know the girls were offering more than escort services?'

'That was between the girls and the client. We never interfered with their ability to earn a little money on the side.' Laurelle looked away as she spoke. She was starting to sound like a corporate spokesman and I wasn't that easy to fool.

'Let's say everything you tell me is true, what about the drivers who took the great and the good to the warehouse last night. How does that work?'

'I had to set that up and find someone to cover for Patrice, we always use different drivers to pick up the corporate clients, clubs and groups, everyone in separate cars.'

'Now I want you to think long and hard about anyone who went rogue, got onto drugs, left without notice or just vanished. Now I can ask Eddie to drag out a list, but my guess is you know off the top of your head who didn't make it home. Laurelle, you know if you ever had a parent with a beef, or a boyfriend who trashed your place looking for answers.' I looked toward the lounge where Eddie was probably working on it now anyway. If it comes from you it will look better to the superintendent, you know that.'

She nodded and looked down. We waited, but she said nothing.

'It will be easier if you tell him, dear.' Donna had this routine worked out.

'We only lost one girl. I thought her mother pulled her out or something,' she wiped her eyes, 'I asked the client, but he said she never showed. I knew her parents were having trouble making ends meet on their farm and I think they hoped Brigitte's looks would get her some modelling work and pull the farm out of debt, but that was years ago.' She reached for the bottle, filled her glass and swallowed hard.

'Who was the client?' I probably said it with more force than necessary, but I didn't care. It might be important.'

'I don't know, but Estelle did.'

'Don't know, or don't remember?' I slapped the table again, aware now of a sharp pain in the heel of my hand. She jumped, 'you said you asked the client.'

'I think you can remember, Laurelle,' Donna was almost singing the question. I decided to watch and wait for a while, 'maybe you think it's too painful and your memory has suppressed it.'

'Oh, I remember.' She began to cry and the words were more stutter than anything cohesive. 'The client was a business man, a guest of the Armenian Embassy. He asked for the youngest girl we had, a virgin.'

'And that was Brigitte?' My temper rose and I fought to control it.

'Yes.'

'What was her surname? You have to remember that.'

'Brigitte, um, Brigitte Collins.'

'On it,' Eddie called from the other room. and I stared at Laurelle. 'can you give me an approximate date?'

'October 2008,' I could see the apprehension in her eyes now, 'Estelle coached her for days.' Laurelle was now, a complete mess, any work that mask had done was worthless now. 'She told her every girl had to have a first time. She wanted her to be prepared.'

'How old was Brigitte?' Donna asked.

'Her mother told us she was seventeen, but I don't think she was much more than fifteen.'

'And my daughter knew this?'

'Yes,' more whisky went into the glass. I took the bottle away from her. Anymore to drink and she'd be no good to anyone. She turned to Donna, her words running so fast I strained to take them in, 'I don't know if it's true, or not, but Estelle told me that Luke Peters once sold her services to a Japanese business man. Apparently, he received over a quarter of a million dollars to spend just one night with him. From that night on, Estelle told me, if she was going to be sold as a whore, it would be on her terms. I think that's when she decided to make an offer for my business.'

'It's okay dear, what happened next?' Donna had those big doe eyes of hers sucking information from Laurelle like a spider sucks the life from its prey.

'To Estelle?'

She powered on, even though what she was hearing must have been tearing her up inside. 'No Dear, to Brigitte.'

'I don't know, we told everyone we thought she was working for an overseas agency. We didn't know what happened and the Embassy stopped taking our calls.'

'And they have never asked for a girl to escort a gentleman again?' Donna prompted, to ease Laurelle into divulging more.

'Never.'

Eddie bounced back into the room. 'Brigitte Collins missing from her home October tenth 2008, listed as a missing person on the eleventh. Police Superintendent Richard Stirling faced the press and said they were doing everything they could to locate her. However, he issued a caveat, telling reporters that officers in charge of the operation suspected the girl was a runaway and possibly in the company of a man of Eastern European descent.'

I looked at him. 'Eight years is a long time to lose a child, what about the parents?'

'The mother died from cancer three years ago. The father lived on the farm until last month when he suicided. No social media. No internet connection. Clean record, not even a parking ticket. He spent most of his time in the outback as a roo shooter. His wife tried out for the Olympic team in 2004 and just missed out.'

'Let me guess,' I said, 'Long rifle?'

'He was champion of his big bore rifle club, too.'

'Opportunity and means. I have to talk to Una or Lucy.'

'Where is he now?'

'Dead. Suicide last month, remember?'

'Sorry,' I said, my mind still trying to take it all in.

CHAPTER TWENTY-EIGHT

Eddie ordered an E.P. Limousine to take us to the police station and it arrived within a few minutes. I assumed Rosen had spread the word, because it seemed I had more influence now than I had when I flashed my police identity. I took Laurelle with me, her testimony was too valuable to risk leaving her at her home or at mine, besides if Tamsyn had told someone about her, I didn't want him shooting anyone near my house. I watched the body language of the driver and it told me he knew Laurelle. However, he chose to stay quiet and she did the same. My only risk was the Assistant Commissioner. I called in a favour and the duty sergeant booked her in as Margaret Windsor, drunk in a public place. I told him no more and he didn't ask. Laurelle knew staying quiet would keep her alive until Lucy or Una came for her.

I burst into Lucy's office and looked at her empty chair.

'She's got a high-profile witness in the interview room. Superintendent Knight is with the other one on room five, but come on sir, you can't be in here, you know that.' The constable was getting agitated. Perhaps, seeing any pending chance of promotion slipping away, he spoke more forcefully, 'I'm sorry Sir, but you know you have to go, the case depends on it.'

'Okay, I'll wait outside, but get a message to either one and tell them I need to see them. Tell them the killer is still at large and I have a theory on who and where.'

'They have them now though, don't they?'

'They have the opportunist yes, but not the killer of the first lot.' I felt the sinews on my neck tighten but held back from crashing their interview. The killer had waited this long, he was either planning his next move or had sated his desire for death. I didn't know. 'Here,' I grabbed a pen from the officer's sleeve, tore a sheet from a pad on his desk, scribbled a note and folded it. He went to look at it. 'Don't read it constable, just deliver it. Una or Lucy, I don't care.'

'Una?' he looked blank

'Superintendent Knight, come on constable, get with the programme, please.'

He ushered me out and disappeared into the building. I sat with the pimps, pushers, drunks and the lonely in a crowded waiting room. I hated it.

Looking at the clock only made my wait seem longer, I swapped to checking the time on my watch. It didn't help. The doors opened, a solicitor and high profile silk wafted in, they didn't even approach the desk where a junior constable was waiting.

'Oh good,' A woman wearing little more than a good-sized handkerchief, called. 'you boys here to bail me?'

The constable guided them deeper into the building.

'Piss off then,' the woman called, 'too pissed and too poor for a pair of pricks like you to even look at, am I?'

I guessed the Assistant Commissioner and his wife had lawyered up. I was about to send Lucy a text. I didn't need to.

'What's so bloody urgent, Voss? Everyone is up to their ears in it here.'

'Laurelle's in the cells, she has information to add weight to the charges you have on Richard Stirling.'

'He's out.'

'The silks that just went past me?'

'It's not always about you though, is it Voss? The Assistant Commissioner has an alibi for the time of the shootings. We're to wrap this case up and I have orders to bring you in.' Her voice flatlined to professional mode.' Sam Voss, I'm placing you under arrest for the murders of Stephanie Simms, Julie Finch and Leah Rose. You are not obliged to say or do anything unless you wish to do so, but whatever you say or do may be used in evidence. Do you understand?'

I knew this caution as intimately as my own name. I could recite it in my sleep, yet I never expected to hear it stated with me as the suspect. 'Yeah, yeah, just get me into an interview room.' I put my hands out. She put cuffs on me and called someone to usher me inside

I sat on the other side of a desk I knew well. The faces of people who'd sat where I was now, flashed like a movie in my mind; pretty people, ugly people, the mad, the sad and the just plain bad, I'd seen them all. The methods used to kill and maim made me sick to my soul, but I'd had to sit there, poker faced, while they spilled their guts, or not, as the case often had been with the non-talkers. There'd once been a theory that women were prolific with poison as their first choice of weapon. Not the ones who'd sat on the side of the table I now found myself on. They'd used guns and knives, one had even used the leg of a chair on a rope and kept turning until her abusive husband gasped his last. The men, tough, nasty, grizzly, full time crims, some of whom just wanted to kill everyone and anyone. Then there were blokes, weak bastards who murdered their wives because their new girlfriend had told them to. Had I seen enough? Probably, but I knew nothing other than police work.

I closed my eyes and hunted for a few minutes of rest. I'd meant to ask Eddie for the father's name, it always helped when negotiators could use the familiar. Una could drag it from the records, before we left.

I stood up and looked around the room, too agitated to just sit. This was not like me, in the past I had been able to use my breathing to control my heart rate, but right now I was trying to calm myself. The cuffs were tight and cut into my wrists when I moved. I smiled at the camera, whoever was watching might as well see I was pissed off. I stared at it a little longer and cleared my throat, noticing the red standby light didn't flash. I looked for the recorder that sat within reach of the interviewer. It was missing. I turned and glared out at the mirrored window. I might even have put my hands to my face and pulled the corners of my mouth out, like I had as a kid, but I was in cuffs. I turned the chair so my back was to the window and tried to sit as comfortably as I could.

The picture of those silks flashing upstairs triggered my imagination. Who were they here to see? Then I shook the image from my head. What if Stirling got to the killer first, would his problems still be there? He'd have had to find someone who was a similar build and couldn't account for their whereabouts when the girls were murdered.

What weapon had been used? Mark said no-one in the hotel had reported anything unusual. Julie, Leah, or Steph had known the shooter. Who could he have found to hang that on? There were too many things that didn't add up. If Una didn't hurry, we were going to have another killing.

The boredom taking its toll, I began to zone out, I must have dozed for a couple of minutes before being startled by a folder slapping onto the desk

'Worked it out yet?' Lucy was removing the handcuffs.

'Worked what out?'

'You're in the frame.' Una was nearly smiling.

'What, how?'

'The Assistant Commissioner told us he saw you coming from the hotel,' Lucy was grinning, 'said you'd greyed your hair and used a false moustache.'

'Grey hair would be good and I only do the tache for Movember,' I started to laugh. 'Do I need an alibi?'

'Got one?' Una lifted one perfectly drawn eyebrow.

'You know I do.' I rubbed my wrists in search of circulation. 'So why arrest me?'

'We had a briefing upstairs and needed you out of the way for a while,' Lucy said, 'Last night someone kicked over a hornet's nest.'

'We're about the only people who didn't get an invite, I wonder why that was?' Una said and leaning both hands onto the desk until her face was almost touching mine. asked. 'Now what's this about a woman in the cells and another murder?' Any levity the room may have held had faded.

'Somewhere in your files, there's a missing person's report on a Brigitte Collins that was treated as a runaway case,' I grabbed a tissue rubbed and dabbed at my forehead, before I realised how much this case was getting at me. 'The parents were fobbed off and didn't understand why. Talk to Laurelle, she can tell you everything, but I reckon the killer has one more intended victim at least.'

'Who?' Lucy checked her iPad.

'I don't know yet, the father suicided a few weeks back and his wife died of cancer six years ago.'

'You think it's someone connected to Collins?' Una was looking at the screen, too.

'Eddie did a search, it eliminated all variables and he came up with that as the only probability.'

'Got it. Garry Collins and wife Dianne reported their fifteen-year-old daughter Brigitte missing tenth October

2008.' She scrolled down a couple of pages. 'Wife died of cancer six years ago. Police were called to a suicide on the family farm almost two months back. So Voss, who do you have in mind for your next hunch? Now I have to ask you to leave, because we have an arrest to make.

'Who?'

'The Assistant Commissioner,' Una smiled, 'forensics have confirmed your service pistol was the weapon used and video evidence showed him taking it from the armoury. We know you were either in the air or in Western Australia at the time of the shootings. So it couldn't have been you. I'll get someone to take you home.'

'Oh, no you don't, I don't want the credit, but I do want to see you arrest this prick.'

'You can watch it. The minister has requested for Lucy to make the arrest. We agreed, and the place is to be crawling with television crews.'

'That's fucking stupid.' My hand went over my head again and I wiped it on my trousers. 'Do you want to get her killed too?' I grabbed Una's arm. 'The bastard's desperate. He's killed three women without care. Do you really think he's going to just give in?' I looked at Lucy and stared deep into her eyes. I wanted her to see my concern for her. 'You go in there and you won't come out alive. Don't do it.'

'We've been over this. I know the layout of the house and I have my story rehearsed. Una will let me know when the TV crews are outside, and then I'll make the arrest, read him his rights and walk him out.'

'I'm telling you no.'

'And I'm saying yes. Think Voss, this will probably be the biggest arrest of my career and I'm doing it.'

'Una?' I said.

'Looks like she has her mind set, Voss.'

'If this is what modern policing is going to look like, then I'm out. You'll have my resignation in the morning.'

'Promise?' Una was teasing and I knew it, but she read me wrong this time.

'The only way I'll agree though, is if I go with you. Then if this goes belly up, and I'm hoping it won't, I want to be there to take the bastard out.'

'You'll have to stay in the car.' Una grabbed my shoulders and stared at me.

'Only as long as you have the situation in hand.'

'Agreed,' she looked at her watch, 'it's time, get your team together, Lucy.'

CHAPTER TWENTY-NINE

My gut churned. This whole thing was a publicity stunt. Una told me a press release had already been drafted and someone from the Minister for Women's department was angling for information, too. All I could see was Lucy being killed on national television, and for what? A bit of chest thumping by Richard Stirling's political foes.

We stopped at the bottom of a tree lined driveway where press vehicles had lined both sides of the road two intersections back from the police road block. I looked around. Across the road to my left, a neighbour had left a horse float at the bottom of their drive with a for sale sign on it. The thing was full of hay, so I didn't know it was hay or the float they were selling. Grass had grown around the tyres, so I knew it had been there since the last rain.

A silver Porsche was parked to one side of the Stirling's circular driveway, our Assistant Commissioner knew how to live.

'I need a gun,' I said to Una as she sat in the passenger seat and briefed Lucy.

'Voss, if you speak again, you'll go into the paddy wagon and wait it out. Now remember, all you have to do is sit in the car and do nothing, say nothing, think nothing. You're not part of this anymore,' She reached back and thrust a manicured nail into my chest. It hurt, but I didn't flinch. 'got it.'

'A fifteen-year-old girl goes missing and the police do nothing. Are you sure we ought to be remembered for this?'

'Give it a rest Voss,' Lucy had fear in her voice, 'it's going to be hard enough in there, without your voice running commentary in my head. Please let me do this. I'll be okay.'

'I still don't like it.'

'You don't have to,' She twisted in her seat to face me. 'okay?

'Okay,' I said and flopped back in mine.

'Now, give us your hand on it,' Una said.

I reached forward to shake the deal, when both women grabbed my wrist and I felt the clamp of a cuff go around it, the ratchet grinding as the other end manacled me to the steering wheel.

'Done.' Una turned to Lucy, 'he'll be safe here until you get back.

The women got out and eased the doors shut. I saw Lucy slip into the passenger seat of a patrol car. Una disappeared into the back of the tactical response unit's mother ship. I struggled into the front seat and tried to release the cuffs. I went for the car keys, but Lucy had taken them. I couldn't get to the glove box to hunt around for a paperclip, or something to pick the lock.

Lucy and her offsider were shown into the house by a woman I thought had to be the wife. Nothing happened for over half an hour and my wrist was almost raw from the cuff. I'd found a pair of binoculars in the console, but everything around the house was in darkness. Sometimes I thought I could see something move, it could have been the wind or one of the tactical response team. I tried every knob and dial on the radios but Lucy had shut everything down. In hindsight, being at home would have been easier, at least I would have had Eddie to let me know who was where.

I found an urgent need to relieve myself and steadied, knowing this was just nerves. I told my body that I could think the feeling away. I looked at my watch, only five minutes had passed since I last looked. I saw a sliver of light at the edge of a front window, someone was probably checking to see the size of the audience outside. It closed again and the house went black.

A movement from the veranda caused the sensor lights to flash and I scanned the garden with the binoculars. A cat chasing moths. It probably did it every night. I relaxed.

A knock on the roof made me flex forward. 'I see you managed to get into the driver's seat then,' Una was at the door, 'Lucy's made the arrest and read him his rights. He's not a happy little dicky bird right now, but tactical response has people stationed all around the house. It's all going as planned.'

'Did you consider the cat in those plans?'

'Being a smartarse doesn't help the situation, Voss.'

'Just get this over the line and I'll retract every comment.'

'You care about her, don't you?'

'Like a sister Ma'am, like a sister.'

'Fuck off.'

The heat of silence from Una was unbearable, but I willed myself to stay quiet. We stayed there staring at the door, waiting for something to happen. It felt like hours had passed since we arrived and I wiped the tension from my head again before leaning back in the seat. Una had her back against the door.

In the end the waiting must have got to her and patience never being one of her strong points, she said. 'I'm going to see what's happening,'

'Get these cuffs off me first.'

'I can't. Lucy's request.'

'You're going to get her killed.' I wanted to say more when the sound of a gunshot came from inside the house. A woman screamed and there was more shouting, the neighbourhood dogs started barking and front lights flooded the street.

'Sorry, gotta go.'

'I'm holding you responsible if anything happens to her.' I shouted at Una's disappearing back.

I wondered about the Collins girl. She'd been fifteen when she went missing, but according to Laurelle, the mother insisted the girl had been seventeen. Collins was dead before the murders started, so we could rule him out. My phone was in my hip pocket and I contorted and stretched until my fingers prised it away. In my enthusiasm, I dropped it down beside the console. Having my right hand shackled to the steering wheel made my search difficult and fat hands made the task near impossible. Once retrieved, I sent Eddie a text asking him to look into the Collins family and if there were any surviving relatives still in and around Canberra.

I watched the driveway and checked my watch again. This was taking too long. The phone vibrated in my hand. Eddie. There had been two Collins children, Brigitte and William. William was almost nine when his sister vanished and was later sent to live with an Uncle Leo in Winton. He returned home for his father's funeral and went back the following week. Other than the uncle, he had no other living relatives. Eddie had found or constructed a meme with wiggling eyebrows to attach. I wasn't impressed. It wasn't the time for levity

The outside lights flicked on and I thought I'd see the bloody cat again. This time, Richard Stirling stood in the doorway of his house, Lucy in front of him as a shield.

This was exactly what I'd been afraid of. In his right hand, he held a gun pressed against her temple. All this was happening and I was shackled to the steering wheel of a police car. I wanted to shout, curse, kick and smash something, but I could do nothing but watch it unfold.

I dropped the phone into my lap and fumbled for the binoculars, focussing them and watched Stirling mouth, 'I need a car and safe passage...'

His words stopped as a shot split the night. A red dot formed on his forehead and he fell to the ground, dragging Lucy with him but, before she could properly stand a woman, who I'd assumed to be his wife, grabbed her from behind and put a different handgun to her head.

Another shot rang out. This time it came from my left, but it sounded to be of a different calibre. I watched a spray of red fill the hallway and then it was gone.

My view of Lucy was hidden as armed officers and police vehicles converged on the house. Emergency sirens and lights filled the area.

The phone vibrated and I picked it up. Another text from Eddie. The uncle had a roo processing business and the Collins kid worked there after school skinning and boning, sending home the few dollars he made. Leo was in hospital with a bowel infection and hadn't seen Billy since his admission.

I wondered about the father's will and returned a text asking Eddie to uncover its detail and get some idea to the value of the Collin's estate. I searched my mind for memories about the case of the missing girl. It was vague, but I remembered Stirling had put a couple of junior officers on it, passing it off as something to test them on. The bastard had been running interference, protecting someone and it wasn't only Estelle. The girl's disappearance was a much bigger case and he'd covered it up. A dirty cop hiding someone's secrets, the same behaviour that ultimately got him killed. I sent another text to Eddie asking him and Donna to scour every financial record he could find on the Stirlings.

There was a thump, a bale of hay fell to the ground and the slim figure of a boy slid down the back of the horse float. He wandered over to my open window. With all attention on the house, no one had noticed him immediately.

'What do I do now?' He asked, putting two rifle bolts on the bonnet of the car.

It was hard to see past him and I could hear footsteps running our way.

'Put your hands on the roof and stand with your legs spread. No-one's going to hurt you.'

'What happened Voss?' Una had her gun drawn and was shouting as she ran toward us. 'Who did the shooting?'

'What's your name son?' I asked.

'William, but everyone calls me Billy, Billy Collins.' He looked confused and angry at the same time, 'That bastard just stood by when my sister went missing and he let my parents die. If they couldn't live with what happened, then neither should he.' He was shaking, although I couldn't tell if this was a winding down of adrenalin or the beginning of a release of long pent up emotion.

Una pulled his hands behind his back and cuffed him. 'Paramedic over here,' she yelled the order, 'now.' She pulled the back door open and thrust him inside. 'I'll deal with you later.'

'He's...'

'Shut it Voss,' she reached in and sprung my cuffs loose. 'get in the back seat and keep him company while I check on Lucy.'

The kid looked at me and shrugged as I slid in beside him.

CHAPTER THIRTY

Billy and I sat in silence. My phone vibrated again and I looked at the screen.

'Here,' I found a jacket on the parcel shelf and pulled it over his head, 'a TV crew has sent a drone up. They'll be trying to get pictures and you don't need that right now.' I kept my head lowered too, and returned a text asking Eddie if he could do something about it. The drone's spot light drilled through the dark. illuminating the inside of the car, but its hovering only lasted a moment before it looped over the trees and crashed onto the roadway ahead of us. Two constables retrieved it.

Emergency vehicles crowded Stirling's front yard and I could see a couple of the forensic team measuring the distance from the steps of the house to the horse float. Billy watched them too.

'Two hundred and twenty-seven metres,' he said.

'Pardon?' I pushed record on my phone.

Billy pointed at someone pushing a measuring wheel down the drive. 'That's the distance. I needed to calculate to set the sight of the big rifle,' He shot me a smile. 'not bad for open sights, eh?'

'But why didn't you go to the police? Why destroy your own life to shoot scum like him?' I shook my head. 'I don't understand. You shoot two people and then you just saunter across and give yourself up. Why?'

'I had the motive, the means and the opportunity, yeah? And now it's done.'

'Yeah, but why say it's over now? Richard Stirling didn't kill your sister. He may not have looked for her, but that just means he's incompetent, it doesn't make him guilty.'

'Yeah, well I'm never going to be able to find that Armenian prick, am I?' He looked at his feet, 'I don't even have a passport.'

'Who and what makes you think he was Armenian?'

'Everything's still at home, it's in all of Mum's letters to that fucking modelling agency and plenty of other stuff among Dad's documents.'

While I listened, I sent a text asking Eddie to check for an Armenian connection.

'Fuck, when you look around our place, the whole bloody house is a shrine to my sister,' he wriggled in his seat, 'and they only kept two photos of me. Why send an eight-year-old kid to dried up, fucking Winton and make him live with a bloke who does nothing but turn roos and other dead shit into dog food. All he does is work and drink piss.'

His words had an edge that I found hard to analyse.

'Only fucking eight and I'm not allowed to miss or grieve for my sister, every time I cried, or showed weakness, good old Uncle Leo sent me out to slaughter a goat, or a sheep, or something. Put an eight-inch knife in my hand and made me cut its throat. I've killed so much stuff that I've become numb to death. I don't feel anything anymore.' His voice was flint hard. 'At first it was the cats and dogs that upset me most. Leo encouraged people bring their unwanted pets in. Oh he told them he'd do it humanely, but in the end, it was just me and the knife. A bloke brought in six greyhounds once. They ended up as pet food too.'

'So why now, why wait?'

'I could get away now. Leo went into hospital, so I walked out. Caught the train to Brisbane, found a flight to Canberra and hitch hiked home. I started going through the bank statements and stuff. I found huge payments going into Mum's bank account. I'm in Winton living and working to send them money because they were living on nothing, but her statements said she was a millionaire.'

'These payments, where did they come from?'

'Dunno. I asked the bank but they wouldn't say because the executors still control her estate.' He kicked the back of the passenger seat. 'I'm up in the stench and the heat, busting a gut for Uncle Leo and getting seven dollars an hour. Skipping school when we were busy and Mum has thousands of dollars coming from somewhere every six months.'

'Do you know when the payments started?'

'Six months after that night Brigitte didn't come home,' he looked past me and to the scene in Stirling's driveway, 'I found some documents in amongst Mum's stuff and there was a modelling contract saying Brigitte was seventeen when they signed it. I knew that had to be bullshit because she only had her fifteenth birthday that July. Fucking lies, everyone telling lies, Mum letting me think Brigitte ran away because of the money trouble Dad was in.' He shuffled around again. 'Can't afford this, can't afford that, because they were saving to go to the Olympics.'

'So, your Dad had money trouble, yeah?'

'That's a parent's excuse for everything isn't it,' his voice mimicked a woman's, *"No school excursion, William, you know we can't afford it."*

'Sometimes that's the way it is, though. All parents want to provide a good life for their kids.' I tried to offer some comfort.

'Not mine. All they wanted was to be Olympians. Anything less than a gold medal was a fail, or that's what they drilled into us. All I wanted was to go to school and have a life and be a normal kid. Instead I'm dumped on a piss-head roo shooter.'

'How did you find the Peters?'

'I looked on the internet and found where they lived. I only wanted some answers about Brigitte, I phoned the woman and asked if she'd see me. She said I could meet her at her husband's office,' He squirmed against the pressure of his handcuffs. 'when I went there, I didn't go in because of Tamsyn.'

'Tamsyn, you knew her?'

'Yeah, she'd been one of Brigitte's friends. They'd gone to school together.'

'And Mr Peters, he's a pretty big bloke, how did you overpower him?'

'I reckon no one wants to die, so I took a couple of Dad's handguns with me.' He shook his head as if to dislodge the memory, 'Tying her up was a bit harder, but I'm stronger than I look.'

A post-mortem picture of Luke Peters flashed in my memory. 'Why kill them though, and why torture the husband?'

Billy gave me a bit of a sneer, put his head back and closed his eyes. Something in his memory must have startled him because he trembled and sprung them open again. 'What a pussy. He kept saying he didn't know anything and every time I cut him, Mrs Peters laughed. She was like an old witch cackling. The woman gave me the creeps, all the time she was saying, "*Reap what you've sown you bastard, reap what you've sown*". I didn't get it.'

'The cut that killed him was the one with a different knife, why?'

He tried to shrug. 'My box cutter broke, had to find something else.'

'So, you just killed them. That easy, eh?'

'I didn't find out what I needed though, did I?' This time he did shrug. 'Then I see you coppers all over the place and at Tamsyn's office. I went back and asked her about it. She knew enough for me to work out what happened. I told her what I'd done to her boss and she just laughed at me. I wanted to know why she hadn't told the police what she knew about Brigitte. She told me she'd taken money to stay quiet. Well, Tamsyn can't tell anyone anything now, can she?'

Una knocked on the window and beckoned me out of the car.

As I got out I said, 'Ask for the best lawyer you can get Billy, you're going to need it.'

He just grinned at me. 'Kids my age can't be tried for murder, I'll be okay.'

I wasn't so sure, but said nothing to damage his confidence.

'Out,' Una was not happy.

'Coming,' I said and opened the door.

'Lucy's asking for you,' she thrust her finger toward a row of flashing lights, 'the second ambulance, you better get over there.'

Lucy was covered in blood as paramedics looked to be monitoring her heart rate and oxygen levels. I could see she was shaken and the blood coagulated on her face was freaking her out, but I didn't think there was anything physically wrong with her.

She lifted her head from the pillow and tried to roll up onto an elbow. 'The boss says you got him.' A paramedic put a hand on her shoulder and suggested she lay down. 'He could have killed me.'

'I don't think so. He was only interested in the Assistant Commissioner and he is a crack shot.' Her hand felt cold and I could feel her shivering.

'How far away was he?'

'Just under three hundred meters,' I smiled, 'open sights too.'

'But why? Why did he shoot?'

'It seems Stirling covered up the disappearance of his sister.'

A paramedic tapped my shoulder, 'Sorry sir, we have to go.'

'I want a full witness report on my desk tonight, Voss,' Lucy called as they closed the doors and the engine started.

Una was standing beside me. 'Forensics says he used two guns, a single shot range rifle and a triple two with a scope.' She took me back to the car and we leant against the front of it staring at the horse-float. 'What did he say to you?'

'Probably the same stuff he'll tell you. He knew he had no hope of finding the people who took his sister, or where she went. He reckons she's dead and a guest of the Armenian Embassy is responsible. Lucy asked me to write it up.'

'Better get on with it then.' she went to walk away, but I caught her arm.

'Ask him how he found the chauffer and why he had to die. Ask the same about Adderton.' Billy claimed to have been acting alone, but it needed to be clarified just how many murders were at his hand and why.

'I'll do it at the station and in my own good time.'

'Don't be so fucking stupid. He's talkative now. You couldn't shut him up if you tried, so ask him while he's still happy to share.'

'I can do this, Voss, I can do this.'

'You're trying to convince yourself Ma-am, not me.' I said.

'Piss off you smug bastard. I'll talk to you later.'

CHAPTER THIRTY-ONE

It was past midnight by the time Una met me in her office, after spending the past few hours interrogating Billy. That had given me enough time at home to precis the information Eddie and Donna had found on the Collins family finances.

Young Billy had been diligent, transferring half his wages home to his father's bank account every month. An account which had remained untouched since Billy's first payment and now held a reasonable sum. Before Brigette disappeared, their business account had been the source of their biggest debt, now the credit balance had ballooned to six figures.

Six weeks before Brigitte went missing, Dianne Collins and her daughter had set up a joint account in the Cayman Islands with a ten-thousand-dollar deposit from Estelle International.

Every half year anniversary another fifty thousand dollars has been transferred into it from another Cayman Island bank account. Eddie couldn't be sure, but thought it likely the funds could be traced back to the European arm of Estelle International. This account too had never been touched.

Forensics later found a box of unposted letters Dianne Collins had written to her daughter, in which she'd said how sorry she'd been for convincing her daughter to sell her virginity just to help the family Olympic ambitions.

Every letter said how she knew now that the Armenian business man's money hadn't been worth it. The team guessed Billy had decided that if the perpetrator was unreachable, then the others involved would pay.

'He's just a kid,' Una said, 'how does anyone that young become that bitter?'

'Years of rejection and deceit poisoned the kid's mind.' I said, as I sat down in the visitor's chair and passed her my statement. 'A family lost, a not so nice uncle and then to find out it was all so unnecessary. I don't know how anyone would handle it.'

'You did,' she said and took the paperwork.

'True.'

'Quite a price to pay for taking someone's innocence though, isn't it?'

I just shrugged. 'Not much innocence to be found here?' I passed her another sheet of paper.

'What's this?' she stared at my letter of resignation.

'Read it.' I smiled at her, blew a kiss and walked away.

AKNOWLEDGEMENTS

The life of a writer is often reclusive, secretive and sombre. There are long periods when they retreat like a rabbit to their burrow, only to emerge as hunger drives them to socialise with family. My wife Ruth, is at the frontline of this vagueness and this book is possible because of her support.

There are others who have helped bring Voss to life. My writing group, Wordsmiths of Melton were excited by the story idea when I presented a first chapter for critique. From that moment it was as if someone lit the touch paper and they carried me as my story developed. Every Wednesday they encourage me to write more, their critiques showing me how to make the story better. So, to everyone in the group, thank you for making my Wednesdays fun.

For me, Merlene Fawdry my writing mentor, coach, and friend is the ultimate editor. Merlene continues to drain the bog of words that slow the reading. She offers suggestions to add glitter and depth to my characters. With a keen eye on the plot, she points me to make changes that will make the reader's experience better. Thank you Merlene, it's easier to write knowing you are there to guide me.

Without a reader, this writing lark would never be this much fun. To have my stories read and enjoyed is the best excuse I use to avoid getting tied to a real job. Thank you to everyone who has read a yarn of mine and I'm sure you will enjoy my first *VOSS* book, *The Price of Innocence,* too.

In His Own Words

Before this case and at a rehabilitation workshop for young offenders, DI Sam Voss introduced himself in this way.

Good morning, my name is Detective Inspector Voss and, I catch killers.

Born sometime in the winter of 1968 at five days old I was left on the steps of a South Melbourne Police Station. All they had to identify me was the beer box that served as a bassinette, a Jack Daniels bottle full of formula or breast milk, no one bothered to test it and a copy of Patrick White's Voss. Desk Sergeant Vaughn Samson took care of me until child services arrived, when the paper work was finished I'd been tagged Samson Voss, a Christian name I've hated ever since. I allow friends to call me Sam, but not often.

A weak and ugly child I was overlooked by many and loved by none. After years of living in an endless roster of foster homes, I became convinced I was always destined to be an outsider. This coupled with a roster of never-ending fights either with teachers, Nuns or anyone of authority I came to believe their suggestions that I was born of the Devil's spawn. For years, those bastards made me feel despised and unworthy.

I believed I was bad until the day I asked a priest in a tattered cassock to describe evil. That old German asked me why I had posed such a question and I told him. In a quiet yet firm voice he dismissed any notion that my birth had been the work of Satan. And those who said it, were peddling rubbish. Every child is born innocent he said, but then he did point out that if I didn't sharpen up soon, I would be headed for death or gaol. He clapped a hand on my shoulder and told me only I could decide.

Neither of those options held a lot of hope, or interest and over the next few years he guided me, pushing, prodding, challenging me to do better.

Father John didn't care how shabby he looked or if his clothes were worn and tattered. He cared for people, street people, working girls the poor and the wealthy. It didn't matter, in his eyes everyone was the same. It's why I'm standing here in front of you today, because he taught me to care. To him, it didn't matter where people came from. It was where they could go that excited him, he knew people could fall or fly and that the choice was theirs.

I took that chance and when I turned seventeen, he passed me into the care of the police academy and I finally found a place I could not only fit into, but somewhere to belong. I found something I was good at and it has provided me with a career that interests me. I had a place to learn about structure. Not just about how a building is put together, or what makes men and women different, but everyday structure. Rules that you may not like, but they are the very framework that a free society is built on.

So, as, a seasoned and accomplished police officer who is determined to put offenders and killers behind bars I stand here before you today asking you Father John's same question. Do you want to fall, or do you want to fly? Because, that choice is yours.

ABOUT THE AUTHOR

Melbourne based novelist Terry L Probert has a background in sales and marketing. Turning to fiction in 2008, his first writing achievement came with Banib the Bunyip, which earned a second prize in the 2013 City of Melton Short Story Competition. The same year, his debut novel Kundela received a Commended in the F.A.W. Christina Stead Awards. His short story, Teenage Summer, is based on a memory from his childhood and was published in The Australian Writer's first quarter edition of 2015.

OTHER TITLES

KUNDELA

'The deft interweaving of indigenous beliefs and human relationships provide added depth and colour to a story that is primarily about past deeds and old enemies – action packed all the way through!'

Sarah Gardener - Moorabool News

GILLESPIE'S GOLD *Planned for release: Late 2018*

Crooked miners and corrupt politicians believe a gold reef exists somewhere on Joe Gillespie's South Australian farm. A failed attempt to eliminate him last year has made them even more prepared to do whatever it takes to stake their claim before he knows it's there.

www.ingramcontent.com/pod-product-compliance
Lightning Source LLC
Chambersburg PA
CBHW030643110726
47901CB00002B/551